Hen
goe

For Nicky,

Best wishes

Vincent

A NOTE ON THE AUTHOR

Vincent Banville was born in Wexford and worked as a teacher, first in Nigeria and then in Dublin. He is chief fiction reviewer of the *Sunday Press* and author of a novel, *An End to Flight,* that deals with the Biafran war. *Hennessy* is first of a series for young people that also includes *Hennessy Goes West.*

PRAISE FOR *HENNESSY*

"A raw, irreverent and, above all, genuinely comic account of the rough-and-tumble adolescence of a very contemporary Dublin schoolboy."

CHILDREN'S LITERATURE ASSOCIATION OF IRELAND GUIDE

"A colourful and hilarious account."

EVENING HERALD

Vincent Banville

Hennessy
goes west

POOLBEG

First published 1992 by
Poolbeg Press Ltd
Knocksedan House,
Swords, Co Dublin, Ireland

Poolbeg Press receives assistance from
The Arts Council / An Chomhairle Ealaíon, Ireland.

ISBN 1 85371 135 7

Cover design by Judith O'Dwyer
Set by Richard Parfrey in Stone Serif 10/14
Printed by Cox & Wyman Ltd Reading Berks

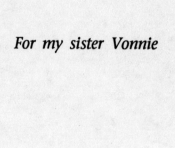

For my sister Vonnie

1

Heuston Station appeared to be in the grip of a riot. There was noise, pandemonium and what seemed to be screams of agony. A seething, pushing mass of humanity expanded and contracted like some huge carnivorous animal doing its best to eat itself.

Most of the individuals concerned were young people, the girls doing the screaming, the boys the shoving. Here and there harassed adults threw their arms in the air and generally gave the impression of being about to do a Pontius Pilate and wash their hands of the whole affair. Over the loudspeaker system a fluting voice, its owner obviously having his or her nose painfully squeezed, announced the times of incoming and departing trains but the language might as well have been Chinese for all the attention it was being paid.

Hennessy stood and surveyed the scene philosophically. His pal Brooks and himself had made a little space for themselves fenced in by their bicycles, but they still swayed in the force of the surge every time a new arrival dived in. "See any sign of them?"

Brooks shaded his eyes, stood on his tippy-toes and rotated through a full three hundred and sixty degrees. "Nothing, captain. Only screaming dervishes as far as the eye can see. Not a sign of a white man..."

"There're going to be deaths when the train pulls in," Hennessy said gloomily. "It'll be like a stampede of maddened bullocks. Some of them are bound to spill over onto the tracks and be run over."

"One way we'll get seats," Brooks responded unfeelingly.

"There is that, I suppose."

It was the first week in July, the exams were over and the annual exodus to the summer schools was at the beginning of its first, fine careless rapture. When Cromwell, all those years ago, drove easterners towards the west with the cry of "To hell or to Connaught" he had no idea what he was starting. Ever since that time the youth from the Pale, when summer warmed their blood, began to feel the stirrings of ancestral yearnings and took themselves off in droves for a few weeks of destruction and vengeance all along the western seaboard.

A sudden shout went up: "the train, the train..." and the tumult started towards its climax. Frantically holding on to their bicycles, bags and cases, Hennessy and Brooks were carried along in the tidal wave, their feet barely touching the ground, all their powers of concentration focused merely on staying upright.

"Give it 'ere."

A man in a peaked railwayman's cap leaned

down and wrestled Hennessy's bike from him. The last he saw of it, it was being thrown into a tangled mass of its companions in the back of the guard's van.

"Be careful with it," Brooks implored, as he handed up his fifteen-speed, brand-new Raleigh. "I just got it for my birthday."

"Sure, sure," the man said, then he flung it as hard as he could in the direction of the others.

"Hope a cow bites your bum," Brooks told him, but the amateur barbarian was already reaching down for his next victim.

"Did you see what he did?"

Brooks was still indignant as they moved along the platform, peering anxiously into crowded carriage after crowded carriage.

"Leave it out, will you?" Hennessy told him. "There's nothing you can do about it now. Our immediate priority is to get somewhere to sit down. It's a three-hour journey, you know."

"I wonder did Swiftie and O'Brien make it?" Brooks said as he stumped along, his bulk making it easy for him to push people out of his way.

"Here, you go first," Hennessy said, ignoring the question. "When they see you coming they'll think you're going to eat them."

"Thanks very much."

Near the top of the train the crowd was thinner and they were able to squeeze up through a door and into a carriage. Bags, cases and haversacks were everywhere, with people using them to keep places for their friends. A quick flurry of blows was exchanged between two fellows over the proper ownership of a seat but peace was soon restored and honour satisfied when both noses became bloodied.

"Phew," Brooks breathed, "that's heavy territory, man. I wouldn't like to sit in the wrong place. You could be strung up."

In a corner alcove two girls were sprawled, their feet propped on the opposite seats. "What about it, girls?" Hennessy asked them. "We've got Coke, chocolate biscuits, and tapes…"

"What tapes?" the girl on the outside asked but doing her best to look bored. She had tightly curled blonde hair and granny glasses, and she was wearing a tee-shirt with "Iron Maiden" stencilled across it.

"Kylie's 'Enjoy Yourself' and Jason's 'Ten Good Reasons,'" Hennessy told her.

"Hah!"

"You no like?"

"What about 'Seventh Son of a Seventh Son?'"

"Ain't got 'im. How about a choccy biscuit, one for each hand?"

The girl looked at her companion who, sizewise, was in Brooks' class. She had a cheerful face, a bush of black hair and was wearing a voluminous bibbed overall. She made a face and shrugged.

"How do we know you'd share?" the first girl asked. "We could give up the seats, you'd plank yourselves and it'd be 'get stuffed girls and go sing for your supper.'"

"You have my word as a gentleman and as a fully paid-up member of the Boy Scouts of Ireland," Hennessy told her. "I swear on my woggle..."

The plump girl giggled and took her feet down, her companion following her example after a suitable interval.

Brooks hefted his case and with an almighty grunt swung it up on to the overhead rack. It teetered for a moment before settling. All four of them gazed up at it; then the girl with the granny glasses put their fears into words: "You're sure it won't fall down and brain us? It looks as if it weighs a ton. What've you got in it anyway?"

"Oh, a little bit of this and a little bit of that." Brooks didn't seem anxious to pursue the topic. "We are staying for three weeks..."

"Three weeks? You look as if you've come equipped for a year."

"So," Hennessy said, changing the subject, "what part of the wild west are you going to? Dodge City, Tombstone, or Boot Hill?"

"Boot Hill is a graveyard, you chump," the slim girl said. "Everyone knows that."

"You said something about prog?" her companion said, between giggles.

"Prog?"

"Food, glorious food." The girl in the granny glasses glared reproachfully at her friend. "It's all Elsie ever thinks about. Looks as if Jumbo here is on the same wavelength..."

"Hey, hold on there," Brooks said uncomfortably. He was doing his best to avoid the eye of his female counterpart across the way from him.

To a cheer that swept through each carriage like a Mexican Wave, the train suddenly lurched into life, creaking and groaning as though in complaint against being so overcrowded. Anxious parents stood on the platform and waved as their various offspring sailed by, most of them only then awakening to the realisation that they would be shut of them for three glorious weeks. Inside the compartments, the sons and daughters basked blissfully in the anticipation of fun and frolics. And in houses, schools and hostelries in the West of Ireland, the natives braced themselves for the cultural and destructive impact...

Kitty and Elsie, as luck would have it, were also bound for the townland of Tóin le Gaoith, where Hennessy and Brooks were to take up habitation. "Have you been there before?" Hennessy asked, in between doling out chocolate Goldgrain biscuits. To Elsie and Brooks they were like the proverbial drop in the ocean.

"Yeah, last year," Kitty said, daintily brushing crumbs off the front of her tee-shirt. "It's a no-no most of the time but the discos can be good."

"D'you have to speak Irish all the time?"

This time it was Elsie who answered. "If you're caught talking English you'll be sent home," she said, with an exaggerated shiver. "Tommy Ugly is the headmaster and he's always snooping around trying to catch someone out."

"Tommy Ugly?"

"We call him that," Kitty said. "His real name is Thomas P O'Snedley. Or Tomás Pádraig Ó Snadlaí, to give him his full title. It's said he eats only cold porridge, morning, noon and night, and that he swims out before his breakfast to wrestle sharks. He looks like a gorilla..."

"Come on..."

"He does. I went by his house one night and saw him swinging from the chandelier. By one leg..."

The two girls laughed, and Hennessy joined in. Brooks, for some reason, was looking acutely embarrassed.

"What's wrong with your friend?" Kitty asked, breaking off in the middle of a snort. "He looks as if the biscuit before last went down the wrong way."

They all stared at Brooks who gave them a sickly grin.

"I don't know," Hennessy said, frowning at him. He jogged him with his elbow. "What's up?"

"Nothing," Brooks answered, although the way he was fidgeting gave the lie to what he said. He grinned again inanely. "I was just worrying about Swift and O'Brien. They don't seem to have made the train."

"Swift and O'Brien? Who're they?"

"Two friends of ours. They're coming down to play music in a pub. They're great. They're going places, you know."

"Yeah, they're going down to Tóin le Gaoith, if you can call that a place. Not exactly the National Stadium, is it?"

"No," Hennessy admitted, "but you have to start small. U2 were only U before they became 2."

"Very funny."

Hennessy spread his hands. "I try, I try."

"I see you've only two biscuits left," Kitty said, staring fixedly at them. "I presume you're going to be the gentleman you said you were and give them to the ladies?"

"Well, I thought I'd keep them for Swifty and O'Brien. After all, they must be exhausted by now running along beside the train."

"Why would they do that, Henno?" Brooks asked, looking perplexed.

"Too mean to pay the fare?"

Brooks scratched his head. "Seems odd to me."

"I'm joking, I'm joking," Hennessy said, raising his eyes to the heavens. "No need to take everything I say literally. Let's go and look for them." He turned to the girls: "Maybe you'd keep these seats for us? We'll break out the Coke when we come back."

"Don't hold your breath," the girl called Kitty said. "There're a few other fellows on this train...a couple of hundred of 'em."

"Ah, but which of them has got our charm, our good looks and our second packet of chocolate Goldgrain biscuits?"

2

"What second packet of Goldgrain biscuits?"

They were pushing their way along crowded aisles, the carriages swaying as the train went down an incline, then round a bend. Guys and girls sat and sprawled in all kinds of places—one small specimen was lying in the overhead luggage rack. The volume of noise from throats, radios and ghetto-blasters was approaching breakthrough point, and even Charlie Bird would have had difficulty having himself heard above the din.

"Wha'?" Hennessy mouthed, cupping his ear.

"I didn't know we had a second packet of biscuits," Brooks bawled in his ear. "I thought I'd eaten them."

"We haven't and you did," Hennessy bawled back. "I just said that so's they'd keep the seats for us. Here..."—he offered him one of the biscuits he had been holding.

"I thought you were keeping these for Swift and O'Brien?"

"They should be so lucky."

They did the length of the train and began retracing their steps. There was no sign of their two friends.

"They must've turned up late."

"Or not at all. Maybe they got cold feet. I've heard the locals can be choosey about who's allowed to play traditional music."

In the gap between two carriages, where it was quieter, they paused. A character in what looked like a long canvas sack was curled up against the door, his head on a duffel bag. Soft snuffling snores trembled up from him and seemed to hang in the air.

Outside, fields, hedges and the occasional house fled by, and away in the distance the sun sparkled on a sudden mirror sheen of water. They were crossing the flatlands of Kildare, mile upon mile of featureless countryside, nothing to be seen.

"What d'you think of the girls?" Brooks asked, idly knocking his knuckles against the door frame and doing his best to look nonchalant.

"The girls?"

"That Elsie is pretty dishy..."

"Dishy? She's an elephant."

"Aw, come on. I admit she's a big girl but there's no need to say that about her."

"Then what'll I say?"

"You can say what you like but I...ah..."

"Are you trying to tell me you fancy her?"

Hennessy conjured up a mental picture of Elsie and Brooks doing a tango together, the ground rumbling beneath their feet.

"What're you laughing at?"

"Laughing? I'm not laughing..."

"Yes you are, you're smirking. It's very unpleasant

to look at...It makes your face like a prune."

Hennessy did his best to compose his features. "So do you or don't you fancy her?" he asked. "If you do you'd better get to work. A dishy piece like her won't stay unattached for long."

"There, you're at it again," Brooks cried. "You're making fun of me. You're as bad as the rest of them."

"I'm not. It's your persecution complex—it's been activated by lewd thoughts of trotting up and down Elsie's spine in your Niké runners."

"What?" Brooks was outraged. "I don't have any such thoughts. And anyway I haven't got Niké runners..."

"But you'd like to, wouldn't you?" Hennessy said knowingly. "You'd like to get that girl in your arms and give her a big squeeze..."

"What if I would?"

"It's only normal for any red-blooded twenty-stone male." In moving to get out of Brooks' reach, Hennessy inadvertently trod on the feet of their sleeping companion but he merely shook himself and went on snoring.

"I shall say no more," Brooks said loftily. "If you can't be civil when your friend wishes to confide his most secret thoughts to you..."

"Aw Brooksie..." Hennessy put on his sad look but his companion's expression was ice that refused to be melted. "I tell you what," Hennessy went on, "when we go back I'll engage Kitty in conversation and you can have Elsie's full and undivided attention. With your charm she'll soon be putty in your hands..."

"Well, to tell you the truth, that's not the way I see it all. You're much better at that kind of thing than I am, so I thought maybe you'd put in a word for me."

"With Elsie?"

"No, with Madonna. Who d'you think?"

"But supposing she falls for me instead of you? And I mean falls—if she fell on me I'd be squashed flat as a pancake. You'd have to scrape me off the floor with a spatula."

"There you go again..."

"The ways of love are not easy." A new voice suddenly broke in on them, coming from around their feet. Their sleeping companion was no longer in the arms of Morpheus. Long and thin like a rake with clothes on, he stretched and yawned loudly. From his appearance he might recently have been pulled through a bush backwards: his off-blond hair was long, lank and dirty, he was badly in need of a shave and his boots had enough clay on them to accommodate a few drills of potatoes. As he stirred, the waxed coat that covered him from chin to ankles creaked audibly.

Brooks gaped down at him, the love of his life obviously forgotten. As for Hennessy, he grinned delightedly.

"'Vanity of vanities,'" the man said, "'all is vanity.' Ecclesiastes, chapter one: verse two. 'A generation goes and a generation comes, but the earth remains forever.' You haven't got anything to eat on you, have you?"

"Afraid not. But there's a restaurant car further down."

With much creaking and groaning the man got to his feet. Beneath all the grime he looked quite young, probably in his twenties. He must have been at least six foot six in height.

"What's that coat you're wearing made of?" Brooks asked inquisitively. "I've never seen one like it."

"Double waxed gaberdine," the man said proudly. "Guaranteed to ward off the fury of the elements, sticks, stones and bottles, and the laser beams of honest folk's disapproval. When I take it off at night it stands by itself and becomes my abode. Gone through a lot, we have. Then again, if I'm ever really starving, I can eat it. You've heard of hard tack, haven't you...?"

Brooks looked at Hennessy and they both burst out laughing.

"That's it," the tall man said philosophically, "'laugh and the world laughs with you, weep and you weep alone.'"

"We've got to go now," Hennessy said carefully. "We're looking for our friends. You haven't seen them, have you? They'd be carrying musical instruments. Drums and a guitar."

"Drums?"

"Well, maybe not the drums. One of them's thin and fair, the other's got red hair like me, and freckles..."

Their companion put his open hand across his mouth and nose and gazed at them speculatively. "If I do spy them, who shall I say was inquiring after them?" he asked.

"I'm Hennessy and this is Brooks."

"Cosgrave's my name, but in the realms of the ungodly I'm known as Jethro. Down on my luck at the moment but things are sure to take a turn for the better. Bound for glory..."

"I'm sure."

Hennessy and Brooks took their leave, but not without the odd backward glance. Jethro waved amiably at them; then began scratching his back by rubbing it against the door frame behind him.

As they got to the most forward carriage they could see that the seats opposite the girls were occupied. "Well, scrub me momma with a down-beat," Hennessy said as they came abreast of the pair who had taken over their spaces, "if it isn't Swift and O'Brien, the strolling troubadours."

"Hi, guys," Swift greeted them, not in the least surprised at their sudden appearance. "I'd ask youse to sit down but there doesn't seem to be any place for you to plant your bods."

"You've got our seats," Brooks exclaimed indignantly. "We just left them for a minute to go and look for you. That's gratitude..."

O'Brien grinned, his hair and freckles ablaze in a sudden dart of sunshine. Beside him Swift looked lean and hungry, the pallor of his skin an unhealthy pale grey. They were both wearing black leather jackets and stone-washed jeans, with O'Brien's fashionably torn at the knees.

"We figured they were your pals," Kitty explained. "They're grubby enough to match the info."

"Where were you anyway?" Brooks asked. "We looked everywhere for you."

"Oh dear, what can the matter be," Hennessy suddenly sang, "poor Swift and O'Brien were stuck in the lavatory..."

"How'd you know that?" asked a surprised Swift.

"Well, it's easy to put two and two together and make five. We did the whole train, searching for you. You were nowhere to be seen. The only conclusion is that you were up on the roof, outside hanging by your teeth to a window strap or locked in the bog. Anyway, it stands to reason that two cheap-skates like you wouldn't do the decent thing and buy tickets. Ergo, you were in hiding while the guard was doing his duty."

"Good thinking, boy wonder."

Hennessy bowed with mock modesty, then suddenly caught hold of Swift, who was sitting on the outside, and wrestled him out of the seat. As he did so, Brooks, showing a surprising agility for someone of his size, wedged himself in between them and into the inviting space.

"Nice one, Brooksie," O'Brien congratulated him. "Remind me to sign you up for the next series of musical chairs."

For the remainder of the journey Hennessy and

Swift had to be content with sitting on the floor. O'Brien broke out his guitar and they had a session, singing their way towards the west, as the train tunnelled its way across the Central Plain, through lush land until it encountered the wind-whistling stone walls and scrubby fields of Co Galway.

In his little haven of peace and tranquillity between the carriages Jethro Cosgrave had gone back to sleep and was dreaming of wrestling a lion on the shore of Africa.

3

Again a scene of pandemonium, this time at Galway railway station. A flustered-looking man with a stack of lists that kept blowing away in the breeze read out names in a foghorn voice, while around him streams of people eddied and swayed as though he were the very obstacle his voice seemed to be warning them against.

Hennessy and Brooks collected their bicycles, while Swift and O'Brien watched over the rest of the baggage. The machines were all interlocked, a mass of resisting steel and chromium, and tempers were becoming frayed as their owners tried to separate them.

"My poor bike," Brooks lamented, as he lifted it down with tender, loving care. "Only a week old and to be given such treatment..."

Hennessy's was an iron horse, built like a tank. It had belonged to his grandmother, Molly Caskey, and was nearly as old as the lady herself. The saddle was as wide and comfortable as an armchair, and the frame seemed to be made from cast iron. When he tried to pedal it uphill, however, it was like riding into a brick wall.

Outside, buses were stacked nose to tail, ready to spirit the eager travellers away to their various destinations. The two girls, Kitty and Elsie, had already found the one for Tóin le Gaoith and were sitting up in it smirking down at them.

Once again the bicycles had to be given into the care of a man in a peaked cap, this time the driver of the bus. He was standing on the roof tying them to a rack and cursing and blinding so much that the air around him appeared to be a whirl of sparks.

"How'll you get there?" Hennessy asked Swift. "No room for you on this bus; it's as packed as a tin of sardines."

"Oh, we'll hitch," Swift said carelessly. "It's a nice day. No problem."

It was indeed a nice day: in fact, it was a glorious one, with the sun now in the middle of the afternoon still high in the sky. A holiday atmosphere that could almost be felt was abroad and everyone was in high spirits. Except for the bus driver, that is, who was still dancing a jig up on the roof and painting the air with lurid curses.

Suddenly there was a commotion, a great clatter of engine noise and a large cloud of blue-black smoke. This heralded the arrival among them of a most singular contraption: it was an ancient motorbike, painted in red and blue, with soaring "Easy-Rider" handlebars, flanged exhausts and an attached sidecar with a wicked-looking, torpedo-shaped nose.

The figure in the saddle was easily recognisable as Jethro Cosgrave, his height giving him away even though his head was enclosed in a battered helmet with Viking horns and his eyes hidden behind mirror goggles. To complete the outfit he was wearing an off-white, trailing scarf round his neck and, of course, his long waxed coat.

Bobbing like jack-rabbits, fellows and girls hurriedly got out of his way: to fall under those wheels could cause instant oblivion.

He drew up beside Hennessy and company and pushed up his goggles. Already their imprint was visible on his sweaty face.

"I see you really are bound for glory," Hennessy complimented him.

"Yeah, but by way of Barna, Spiddal and other places west. I'll ride till I hit the Atlantic; then I'll take off and disappear into a cloud."

"Like Amelia Earhart?"

"Amelia who?" O'Brien asked, but keeping a safe distance from the growling motorbike.

"Amelia Earhart," Jethro said. "She was a lady aviator who went up once too often and never came down. Your friend shows a surprising knowledge for one so young."

"He's a 45-year-old midget," Swift chimed in. "You wouldn't want to be fooled by appearances."

Jethro saw them looking at the motorbike and he said, "It's a Harley-Davidson Electra Glide. Not too many of them around any more. Completely rebuilt by my own hands and Mac's scrap-metal shop." It was obvious that he was very proud of the machine.

He worked the throttle and the big motorbike lurched forward like a young horse chafing at the bit.

"There's your lift," Hennessy said, grinning at Swift and O'Brien. He turned to Jethro. "These two are looking for a carry out to Tóin le Gaoith," he informed him. "If you're going in that direction maybe you'd do the necessary?"

Ignoring their murderous looks, Hennessy smiled brightly at his two friends.

"Certainly," Jethro said, also choosing to pay no attention to their obvious reluctance. "'With my many chariots I have gone up the heights of the mountains, to the far recesses of Lebanon': Kings, chapter 19: verse 23."

"This guy's a spaceman," O'Brien hissed in Hennessy's ear. "We'd be as safe with him as we would with Evil Knieval."

"Step aboard, gents," the tall stranger on the motorbike encouraged them. "The road awaits..."

"Hope that's all that awaits," Swift muttered, then more loudly he said, "Remember the old motto: 'It's better to arrive late than dead on time.'"

While O'Brien squeezed himself and his guitar into the sidecar, Swift settled himself on the pillion, then tentatively clasped his hands around the driver's waist. The three of them looked like one of those circus acts just before it all goes wrong. As they prepared to move off Hennessy saluted, while Brooks made no attempt to hide his snorts of laughter.

Replacing his goggles with a snap like a knight of old lowering his visor, Jethro twisted the throttle and, to a muffled shout of "Praise the Lord," the ill-assorted trio went charging down the incline and out into Eyre Square. Although quickly lost to view, their progress could be gauged by the blaring of horns and the screeching of brakes. It appeared that Jethro was neither a wise nor a dutiful driver.

Connemara is not that clearly defined a territory but once past the suburbs of Galway city the first whiff of turf smoke signals that one is entering that mythical kingdom.

Once upon a time it was an area of thatched cottages, little stone-marked fields, men in bawneen jackets and trousers, and women in shawls. Gaelic was the dominant, if not the only, language; there was an amount of poverty, but there was also fun and laughter, music and dancing, and an adherence to old ways that formed a bridge between the past and the present.

It is true that a number of the young people had to emigrate but there is a wanderlust ingrained in the Irish character that gives itchy feet no matter what the circumstances, and who is to say that these people would not have gone even if the necessity to do so hadn't been present?

Nowadays modern detached bungalows have sprung up all over the place, the thatched cottage is as commonly seen as the cuckoo and English is in the process of swamping the native tongue. Keeping the seasonal Irish scholars is one of the ways of making money and, because of the need for more and more space, houses that began life by being symmetrical and pleasing to the eye have taken on shapes that defy description. Long barn-like structures extrude from the sides, extra storeys are built on and in some cases the actual owners go off to live in a shed at the bottom of the garden in order to accommodate a few more paying customers.

The living quarters that Hennessy and Brooks were assigned for the duration of their three-week stay were in a house owned by a Miss Ó Fatharta, a pleasant, grey-haired woman who had resisted the urge to ruin her beautiful stonecut cottage by building on an extension. The consequence was that the two of them had a room to themselves, actual beds instead of bunks, and a view down over an inlet of the sea which promised early-morning grandeur that would make waking up a pleasure.

"I bags the one on the left," Brooks said, indicating the bed in the corner as soon as their landlady had left. To assert his ownership he swung his massive case up on to it.

"Why? They're both the same."

"No, this one's wider."

Hennessy measured it critically with his eye. "You're nuts. There's not a bit of difference between them."

"Well, it looks wider to me."

"Whatever you say."

Hennessy unpacked his duffel bag. He did this by turning it upside-down and dumping the contents out on the bed. His Sunday clothes, which consisted of a faded lumberjack shirt and crumpled cords, he hung up in the ancient, brown-stained wardrobe. The smell of mothballs from it made his eyes pop.

When he turned round it was to see Brooks folding back the lid of his case. It was obvious he was trying to hide what was inside by putting his ample bulk in front of it. Pretending to be absorbed in the wallpaper, Hennessy sidled closer until he could get a look at what Brooks was attempting to conceal.

"Holy jumping Joseph, you must be expecting a famine!"

"What?"

Brooks looked around guiltily, then turned to gaze with Hennessy into the suitcase. Instead of clothes, the inside was packed with food: tins of beans and peas, packets of biscuits, cellophane-wrapped slices of cheese, cartons of yoghurt, jars of sweets, bottles of orange juice—there was enough to stock a small shop and still have enough left over to feed a host of ravenous orphans.

"Have you any pig's feet?" Hennessy asked. "Or a few yards of sausages? No wonder the thing weighed a ton. You must've thought you were travelling to the moon."

"Well, you should always be prepared," Brooks said defensively. "I've a big constitution and it takes a lot to feed it..."

"Constitution? Why don't you call a spade a bloody shovel? You've a belly like a June pig."

"Go jump in the lake." Brooks closed the lid of the case with a bang. "And don't come looking to me in the dog-hours of the night for a little something to keep you going until morning. You can go howl at the moon."

"It's you that'll be howling if you eat all that junk. One of these days you'll burst."

"You think so? I bet I'm stronger than you. How about an arm wrestle to prove it?"

"Not on your sweet bippy. The last time I tried that with you my arm was numb to the shoulder for a week. You provide the brawn in this outfit, I'll provide the brains."

Brooks appeared to be about to dispute that when there was a knock at the door and they could hear Miss Ó Fatharta calling them for their tea.

"You hear that?" Hennessy said. "They do have grub around here. You'll have as much use for your tins of beans as a duck has for an umbrella."

"We'll see," Brooks replied. "Better to drown in custard than swim in sour milk. That's the Bible according to Brooks, chapter one: verse one."

4

Miss Ó Fatharta and her ancient father, Micky Pats, were sitting at a table groaning with food. Hennessy gave Brooks an "I-told-you-so" look before they sat down to tuck in.

The woman of the house spoke in Irish but when Brooks, after many stops and starts, told her that Hennessy had as much of the language as an egg, having spent the greater part of his life in Africa, she condescended to speak in English.

"Only until tomorrow now, when the course starts," she explained. "From that time on it'd be as good as my life is worth to speak anything but the Irish. Annaway, you'll have to do likewise yourself. If not, you'll be sent home. Master Ó Snadlaí is verra firm about that."

The old man sat upright in a straight chair and watched everything that went on with a pair of lively brown eyes. They were the only things lively about him; otherwise he was as decrepit as a leaf in autumn. He looked about a hundred years old.

While Brooks burrowed his way through a small mountain of chips, Hennessy gazed about him. The kitchen was furnished in the old way—a tall open dresser with hooks for the cups, chairs with roped straw backs and seats, and an open hearth

complete with a bellows made from an iron wheel
and a taut leather strap to work it.

A black kettle hung over the turf fire, but
otherwise the gleaming Calor gas cooker in one
corner was where the cooking was done. The
stainless steel double sink was also a modern
innovation, as were the fridge-cum-freezer and the
electric kettle and toaster.

"Is that a beach that I saw from the bedroom
window?" Hennessy asked his landlady. "It looked
like one."

"That's Trá na Reilige," Miss Ó Fatharta told
him. "Nice and safe to swim there but you'd want
to be careful of the ghosts be night."

"Ghosts?"

"*Reilig* means 'graveyard,'" Brooks supplied
between mouthfuls.

"Oh."

"I'm only joking," his landlady went on. "Although there's some that do be saying they've seen
odd things when the moon is full."

The old man suddenly cleared his throat and
said something in a thick, phlegmy voice. As though
to emphasise what he had said he then proceeded
to spit in the fire.

"What'd he say?" Hennessy asked, at the same
time moving back out of range.

"Don't be minding him," Miss Ó Fatharta
laughed. "His head is filled with queer notions
about spirits and hobgoblins. He says that at
midnight the fairy folk come out to play..."

"Oh, you've got those around here, too, have you?"

"Not that kind," Brooks whispered. "He means leprechauns and things like that."

"I wouldn't be too sure."

Hennessy nodded in a friendly fashion at the old man but all he got in return was a gleeful cackle. Micky Pats had the look of a bold child who, as soon as the adult back was turned, would throw his morning goody all over the place. He winked at Hennessy, then popped his false teeth in and out with a "now-you-see-them-now-you-don't" quickness. He would bear watching.

After tea, Hennessy and Brooks went out behind the house and down a winding track that led towards the sea. The graveyard was situated on a kind of plateau, small and enclosed, with many crooked tombstones and one huge soaring angel in age-grimed marble. There was a brooding air about the place, the descending sun shooting bloody beams across it as though marking it down for ownership. Above them a lone gull croaked forlornly in the reaches of the sky.

The track curved along by the side of the graveyard, then abruptly ended in a stile that forced them to go through part of it in order to get to the seashore. Brooks hung back, his normally placid face registering a trace of anxiety. "Come on, what's wrong with you?"

Hennessy sat on the stile and looked back at his

friend. Now that the sun was on the wane, there was a chill in the air. Brooks suddenly shivered.

"Someone walk over your grave?" Hennessy inquired unfeelingly.

"What?"

"Well, it's what they say, isn't it?"

"I'm cold, that's all. Why don't we wait till morning to have a look at the beach? See more then..."

"Where's the poet in you?" Hennessy moved his arms windmill-fashion and the glare of evening light behind him made him appear to be flying. "You have to see the sea by twilight's last gleaming. Bet if you put your hand in the water, the drops'd look like liquid silver."

"Really? I'll have you know I intend putting no part of me into the water at this hour of the night. The only time that I'll venture into the sea is when the sun is blazing hot, the lifeguards are poised and I'm wearing water-wings and an inflatable lifejacket."

"You can't swim?"

"I can float."

"About the same thing, isn't it?"

"Not quite. When you float you usually stay in the one place. When you swim you move about a bit. Although once I started floating out to sea, only the tide turned and brought me back in again. I could have drowned."

"Naw, it was like the return of Moby Dick, the great white whale. They've probably written a song about you."

"That's your story, is it?"

"Yes, and I'm sticking to it."

Reluctantly Brooks followed Hennessy over the stile and into the confines of the cemetery. Most of the inhabitants appeared to have died in the last century. The most recently deceased was a Seán Ó Donnchadh, who had fallen asleep in the Lord on the 24th February, 1900. He was reposing under the marble angel, a particularly repulsive specimen with a sneer on its face as though implying heaven was full up and no one else need apply to get in. To Brooks' overheated imagination the eyes of this gargoyle seemed to be following him about as he moved.

Unlike the rest, this grave was actually a cement tomb, quite spacious and with a grilled door at the bottom of the incline leading into it. Hennessy peered between the bars but only darkness was visible. In a sepulchral voice he said, "Arise you spirits of the undead. Arise and follow Charlie..."

"You're too late," Brooks said gloomily, "they're already up in Dublin tramping along behind him."

"Reminds me of that Michael Jackson video... What was it called?"

"*Thriller*."

"Right on."

They moved along, climbed over another stile and were suddenly on a small promontory that overlooked a stretch of beach, piles of seaweed laid out to dry, and a glassy sea that wrinkled gently on to the sand. The very air seemed pink from the descending sun and the quietness could almost be felt. Away across from them the dark outline of another finger of land poked out and tiny pinpricks of moving light traced the progress of cars. Further out again, on the horizon, the on-again, off-again blink of a lighthouse guided mariners safely home.

"Cripes," Brooks breathed.

"Pretty impressive, isn't it?" Hennessy agreed. "If you could bottle the air and sell it you could make a fortune."

"That's the poet in you speaking, is it?"

"You no like? Try this then"—Hennessy took up a dramatic pose, one hand extended, the other cradling his brow:

There is sweet music here that softer falls,
Than petals of blown roses on the grass..."

He paused, then he said, "Would you believe it, I've forgotten the rest..."

"It's very nice anyway," Brooks said. "But I know one too:

There was a young man from Leeds,
Who swallowed a packet of seeds..."

Hennessy stared at him, grimacing. "Charming," he said. "Like a dog lifting his leg in a rose garden."

"Don't be so bolshie then..."

Brooks jumped down onto the soft sand of the beach and shuffled towards the water. He began picking up flat stones and skimming them over the surface. They skipped along leaving ever-widening ripples behind. Hennessy joined him and they competed to see which of them could get a stone to stay up longer.

It was quite dark by now, and they were taken by surprise when the figure of a man in a wet suit and flippers came walking backwards out of the surf. When he turned to face them they could see that his goggles and snorkel had been pushed up onto his forehead.

He greeted them in Irish: "Conas 'tá sibh?" then went on to ask them who they were. Haltingly Brooks introduced himself and Hennessy. Still speaking in Irish, he went on to ask them if they were on the course, then told them that his name was Seán de Burca and that he was one of the teachers.

"You'll have to excuse me," Hennessy told him, "but I've very little of the language. I lived most of my life in Africa, so I didn't have much opportunity of picking it up."

The man grinned, showing white teeth in a dark face. He was young, in his twenties, and he had black curly hair, a strong-featured, handsome face and a tightly muscled body that spoke of long hours of exercising.

"Africa, eh?" he said, switching to English. "What part?"

"West Africa mostly. Nigeria. My father's an engineer."

"Wasn't there a civil war out there sometime in the early 'seventies?"

"That's right. I wasn't even born then but I've heard of it."

"Must be pretty exciting to be caught up in a war. The whiff of danger, that kind of thing..."

"You can have it as far as I'm concerned. A lot of people died back then."

"They usually do, in a war."

de Burca sat down and began taking off his flippers. The light was almost gone and he was little more than a dark presence against the pale glimmer of the sand.

"Maybe you'd better run along," he told them. "Early start tomorrow. The headmaster doesn't like anyone turning up late. So I've been told anyway. I'm new to this kind of thing myself, although I've spent a lot of time in this area."

Brooks, for one, did not need much encouragement to depart. He took off like someone suddenly short-taken, thundering back the way they had come, and he was already looming up in the lighted rectangle of the back door when Hennessy was still only climbing over the second stile. When Brooks had to, he could move as fast as the next man—not gracefully, but fast...

Sometime in the middle of the night Hennessy awoke from a deep sleep and lay trying to get his bearings. In the other bed Brooks was snoring as though practising to play the last trumpet.

Wondering if that was what had awakened him, Hennessy cautiously climbed out on the floor and crept over to the window. He drew aside the curtains and looked out. It was a dark, moonless night, but in the middle distance he could see the sea glinting with starshine.

He was about to turn away when he noticed a light bobbing about in what he surmised must be the graveyard. It was only a brief flicker and he was beginning to think he had imagined it when it suddenly winked on again. About to wake Brooks so that he could confirm that there was a light there, he paused when it went out once more. This time it stayed off.

He remained at the window for a while longer but nothing else disturbed the deep silence of the night except the cacophony of snores from the other bed. When Hennessy had met Brooks for the first time he had introduced himself as a champion farter. It appeared that he was a champion snorer as well.

Before he retired once more, Hennessy tiptoed over to Brooks and stuffed part of the sheet into his open mouth. Then he caught hold of his nose between finger and thumb and squeezed. Nothing happened for about ten seconds, then with a mighty roar Brooks reared up in the bed like Lazarus answering the call.

"Wha's a matter, wha's a matter?" he bellowed, but by this time his room-mate was safely back in his bed and apparently fast asleep.

For the rest of the night Brooks twisted and turned, his mind in turmoil. He was convinced that the angel from the graveyard had come alive, flown in the window and sat on his face.

5

The next morning dawned bright and sunny. Brooks was lying half-in and half-out of the bed, for all the world like someone who had come out second-best in a wrestling match.

Leaving him to his slumbers, Hennessy went down to the beach for a swim. The water literally took his breath away but as his body temperature adapted to it he found it invigorating and refreshing. He swam out into the inlet, doing a fast crawl, then paused, flipped over on to his back and floated with his eyes closed.

After a while he heard a shout and, when he looked, he saw Brooks waving to him from the shore. He swam in and stood on the gently shelving bottom with the water up to his waist. "Come on in," he called. "A swim'll set you up for the day."

"No fear," Brooks answered, shuddering. Hugging himself he said, "I haven't had my breakfast yet. I'm as empty as a drum. A few rashers, a sausage or two, maybe a couple of cartwheels of black pudding...I can taste them already."

"Here, taste this," Hennessy said, and with his open hand he slashed a ragged ribbon of water in the direction of his plump friend.

Brooks was no fool, however: the quickness

with which he dodged suggested that he had been expecting such a move. "You'd want to move faster than that to catch me out," he taunted. "I float like a butterfly, sting like a bee."

"More like Dumbo than a butterfly," Hennessy scoffed.

He came out and began drying himself down. The beach was deserted except for the two of them. From somewhere further out on the peninsula a small boat hove into view, with one lone man in it. It chugged away from them, seeming to glide along its reflection out towards the Aran Islands, distant in the morning haze.

"I wouldn't mind being him," Hennessy said wistfully, indicating the man in the departing craft. "Out on the open sea on a morning such as this. He'll probably see some flying fish."

"Flying fish or frying fish? I think I can hear a few sizzling."

"Always thinking of your gut. Wouldn't you rather spend a few hours tacking about out there than stuffing yourself at the breakfast table? No, don't answer that, I know the answer already."

"Why don't you put a sock in it?" Brooks said. "You're all full of blather. And it's just come to me that it was you who tried to suffocate me during the night. I could've had a seizure."

"It was for your own good."

"What d'you mean?"

"You were fighting a tuba and the tuba was winning."

"Tuba? What tuba?"

"Snoring, you clown. You were snoring to wake the dead. And that reminds me, I think the spirits were having a hoolie down in the *reilig* last night. Either that or you woke them up as well..."

Brooks looked at him. "That's not funny," he said.

"Honest to God, I did see something down there. It was a light and it was moving about for five minutes or so."

"You imagined it."

"No, I didn't. Let's go and have a look."

Hennessy slung his towel scarf-fashion around his neck and set off back towards the graveyard. When he got there he began poking about, looking behind tombstones, tramping down nettles, investigating areas of long grass. He was down peering in through the grilled opening of Seán Ó Donnchadh's crypt when he heard a strangled cry from Brooks.

Returning quickly to the surface, he saw his friend reeling around as though he had been attacked by a swarm of killer bees. "What's the matter?" Hennessy asked him, "Did you see Rover the dog run off with the sausages?"

Brooks, however, appeared to have lost the power of speech. All he could do was moan and point wildly towards a corner of the cemetery. Hennessy followed the direction he was aiming at and beheld a pair of feet sticking out of a clump of bushes. The feet were encased in a pair of dilapidated boots but they indisputably belonged to a human being of some kind. "Holy Moses," Hennessy breathed, a sudden shiver goosing his spine, in spite of the burgeoning heat of the sun.

"Don't go near it," Brooks cried, his voice returning in a rush. "It's a body. We'll have to call the guards. Nothing must be touched..." He sank down on the ground, his back to the sneering angel. "Oh Mammy..."

Hennessy, made of slightly sterner stuff, cautiously approached the feet. They twitched, causing him to rear back in fright. Now that he was closer he could see tweed trouser-legs and they undeniably had a familiar look about them. He parted the bushes and saw the face of Miss Ó Fatharta's aged father, Micky Pats, grinning up at him. The old man was spreadeagled out on a bed of thick, springy grass and looked as happy as a pig in muck.

By this time Brooks had worked up the courage to come closer. "Is he dead?" he asked, still averting his gaze.

Hennessy leaned down and sniffed; then he straightened up again. "He's dead all right," he said. "Dead drunk."

"Wha?"

"He's mangled, twisted, pie-eyed, sozzled, stocious...call it what you will, it still amounts to the same thing. The man's spaced out on the juice of the grape or some such."

"At this time of the morning?"

"He's probably working on the carry-over from the night before. I wonder where he got it?"

"Probably poteen."

"What's that?"

"A kind of gin that they make around here. Fermented from barley, I think. Didn't they have something like that out in Africa?"

"As it happens, they did. It was called *kai-kai* and a shot of it would put you into orbit. Not that I ever tried it but I have it on the best authority that it was dynamite."

They stood and gazed down on Micky Pats, and he grinned back at them, showing off gums and a bright red tongue. Nothing short of an earthquake would disturb him and even then he'd probably only regard it as a minor irritation.

At half past eight they were strolling down the road towards the school when they came across Swift and O'Brien sitting on a stone wall. They looked as if they hadn't slept too well.

"Who's a good boy, then?" Swift said mockingly. "All scrubbed up and ready for a hard day before the blackboard..."

"Leave it out," Hennessy told him. "It's bad enough without you making it worse." He squinted at them in the bright sunshine. "How'd you get on anyway? Fixed up okay?"

"You could say that, I suppose," Swift said, while O'Brien gave a derisive snort.

"Oho, do I detect a hint of unease behind the

finely groomed air of carelessness? Things not work out as you'd hoped?"

"Well, for starters, we had to sleep in a kip that even a tramp'd turn up his nose at," O'Brien said, ignoring his companion's warning shake of the head. "Then we were told that we were on a week's probation. If the customers don't like us we'll be run outta town so fast there'll be skid marks all the way to Dublin."

"You have to be exaggerating."

"Only a little."

"So you're on probation, eh? When's your first session? I wouldn't want to miss that for the world."

Brooks, wearing a flowered Hawaiian shirt and plaid bermudas that made him look like a refugee from an American package tour, raised his eyebrows. "I'm afraid, old skin, that you will miss it," he said.

"How's that again?"

"Pubs are off limits. Didn't you read the set of rules that came with the signing-on form? No drinking, smoking or larking about. The first time you're caught speaking English, you get a warning. The second time it's hands, knees and bumps-a-daisy, and you're off on the rocky road to Dublin. The discipline is tighter than the skin of a drum."

Hennessy frowned and then the light of battle began to form in his eye. "Rules are made to be broken," he said. "I'm not going to mince around saying 'Yes, sir' and 'No, sir' and 'Three bags full, sir.' We have to go and lend our support to Swiftie and Nedser. It wouldn't be right not to."

"There speaks a true blue mate," Swift said approvingly.

"There speaks a true blue lunatic," Brooks muttered. He looked around uneasily as other little knots of fellows and girls went trudging by. "You do anything out of the ordinary and you'll stick out like a sore thumb. I've heard this Tommy Ugly runs a tight ship."

"Then think of yourself as a mutineer."

"And end up walking the plank?"

"Faint heart never won fair maiden."

"What fair maiden?"

"Speak of the devil..."

At that moment Kitty and Elsie came trotting down the road, both of them wearing summer dresses. Kitty had combed out her hair into a semi-Afro, while Elsie, rather spoiling the femininity of the dress, was wearing a pair of shiny brown Doc Martens. Linking arms, they pretended to ignore the presence of the four gawkers standing by the wall.

"How's it going, girls?" Swift inquired, as they came abreast of him.

Kitty sniffed. "Don't mind them riff-raff," she told a giggling Elsie. "Just pretend they're not there."

"Huh, pardon us for living," Hennessy said, tossing his head.

Kitty stuck her nose in the air but Elsie grinned at Brooks, who promptly turned a bright shade of crimson. As they went on down the road he looked longingly after them.

Swift gave O'Brien a nudge, then he said, "I wouldn't mind the fat one. Plenty to squeeze there."

"She's not fat," Brooks protested, rising to the bait. "She's just..."

"Just what?"

"Just you keep your eyes off her, I saw her first."

"The best of luck to you."

To change the subject, Hennessy said, "What happened to Jethro, the guy that gave you the lift?"

The other two groaned in unison. "Did you have to mention him?" Swift asked. "He frightened the living daylights outta us. Bawling out hymns at the top of his voice and driving like a maniac. There were times when I thought we'd take off and come down in the sea."

"Where's he staying?"

"Haven't a clue. As soon as he dumped us, he took off in a cloud of dust. He's probably halfway to paradise by now, if he didn't go in the opposite direction. Why're you interested?"

"No particular reason. He just seemed like a gasser. Might liven up the place a bit."

"'Spect he'll turn up. Spouting fire and brimstone outside the church on Sunday, maybe."

Brooks was getting restive, shuffling his feet and biting his nails. "I suppose we'd better get going," Hennessy said. "Beard the lion in his den. It's well for you fellows. Think of us when you're lying out getting a tan. We'll be inside sitting on a hard old bench, listening to Tommy Ugly telling us how to be good, Irish-speaking citizens. Lucky sods..."

6

The school where the academic side of the course was to be conducted was situated right in the middle of the village. In the paved yard groups of fellows and girls stood, leaned or sat, while in one corner a basketball game was in progress, a few of the participants showing the practised skill of people who played a lot.

At ten minutes to nine a short bald-headed man who looked like Bob Hoskins came out on to the verandah and began ringing a handbell. When he had their attention he started speaking in Irish, spitting it out at a rate of knots as though he had been wound up.

As far as Hennessy was concerned, he might as well have been speaking double Dutch. "What's he on about?" he asked Brooks, but he only scratched his head and shrugged.

A fellow standing nearby, a superior-looking type with an inbuilt sneer, said out of the corner of his mouth, "He's telling us to line up so that we can be inspected for fleas, lice and high water marks around the ears..."

Part of what he said was true, for the assembled mob did shortly begin rearranging itself into straggling lines. When a semblance of order had been established, the school door opened again and a number of adults came out, both male and female, led by a hugely bearded bear of a man wearing a schoolmaster's gown over a white shirt, khaki shorts and knee-length, laced-up boots.

Drawing his little band along in his slipstream, he went up and down the rows of uneasy students, stopping now and then to glare fiercely whenever anything displeased him.

When he came to Brooks he paused and stared disdainfully at his colourful raiment; then he suddenly barked a shower of spit-impregnated words at him. Brooks immediately went a deep shade of puce, put down his head and gazed miserably at the ground.

Luckily for him the fellow who had spoken earlier gave a snort of laughter, an occurrence that immediately caused Father Bear to turn on him, his voice rising from basso profundo to falsetto like a train going into a tunnel. On and on he went, while the rest of the students shifted about uneasily and the little group of adults stared embarrassedly into the middle distance. One of them caught Hennessy's eye and he realised that it was Seán de Burca, the swimmer from the night before. He raised his eyebrows, then winked.

Firing one final warning burst, the man in the gown turned on his heel and stalked off. The sigh of relief from those in his immediate vicinity was like the sound of a giant balloon deflating.

"I take it that that's Tommy Ugly," Hennessy

whispered under his breath to Brooks as they filed into the school building. "He's certainly well named. I saw a few like him out in Africa but they were swinging through the trees."

The rest of the morning was spent in getting the formalities out of the way. Hennessy and Brooks were assigned to Seán de Burca's class, to their relieved satisfaction. He gave them a timetable: lessons in the morning until twelve, excursions, rambles, sports and so on in the afternoons. Most nights there would be a social of some kind, a céilí, a fancy dress, a sing-song or even a disco.

de Burca spoke slowly in Irish but with many an English phrase thrown in. He assured them that as the course progressed, there would be less and less English. He had an easy-going manner about him that thawed out their natural suspicions of authority, and soon the atmosphere in the classroom was cheerful and light hearted.

Hennessy quickly learned off by heart some sentences of greeting, trying them out on Brooks and on Kitty and Elsie who were also in the class. So interested did he become that he was surprised when the lunch bell rang.

As they went back out into the sunshine, there was much horseplay, the man with the list who had rung the bell that morning being quite unable to quell the racket. His name was Ó Cadhla and he was second-in-command to Tommy Ugly. They were an ill-matched pair for, whereas the principal was as fierce as a grizzly with a thorn in his paw, his vice-principal had as much authority about him as a wilting marshmallow.

The afternoon was free in order to give them a chance to explore the village and its surroundings, so Hennessy, at Brooks' instigation, did his best to soft-soap the girls into accompanying them. "So, what d'you say?" he asked Elsie, figuring that she might be the more easily persuaded of the two. "Will we tip around together? Safety in numbers, you know. There could be Indians, wild animals, fellows trying to sell dirty postcards of Tommy Ugly eating his morning porridge..."

Elsie giggled—he would have been surprised if she hadn't. "I suppose so," she said. "But only if you buy us refreshments before and after..."

"Supposing instead of buying, we bring?"

"You mean...?"

"Well, Brooksie's brought along enough provisions to feed an army. He wouldn't miss half a ton of chocolate bars and a few gallons of Coke."

This arrangement appearing to be satisfactory, they made a date to meet at two-thirty and went their respective ways.

As soon as they parted Brooks said testily, "Why'd you have to tell them I brought all that grub? That's private and confidential information."

To mollify him Hennessy said, "Couldn't you see that Elsie was impressed? And wasn't it Napoleon who said that an army marches on its stomach?"

"What's Napoleon got to do with it?"

"Nothing much. I just thought I'd throw that in..."

"...to change the subject. Yeah, I know. You're always doing that to me. Making irreverent statements just to get me confused."

"I think you mean irrelevant."

"Do I? Well, whatever. I'm not as dozy as you imagine..." Brooks kicked a discarded tin can along in front of him. Then he said, "You really think Elsie was impressed? You think the way to win her...ah, affections...is by feeding her face?"

"Well, I wouldn't have put it quite like that but yes, it would make for a definite line of approach. Amazing what effect an éclair oozing cream or a cascade of Cadbury's Irish Roses can have on a girl's powers of resistance. Hey, you'd have her literally eating outta your hand."

Brooks stopped suddenly and glared at Hennessy. "Are you taking the mick or what?" he asked him. "Here I am looking to you to help me in..."

"...an affair of the heart?"

"Something like that." Brooks squeezed his eyes shut, then opened them again. "And all you can do is make fun of me. What kind of a friend are you, anyway?"

"Aw, Brooksie, don't be like that." Hennessy punched him playfully in the shoulder. "You know I've got your best interests at heart. Stick with me, kid, and by the end of the course you and Elsie'll be canoodling like two love-sick elephants..."

Brooks made a grab but by that time Hennessy was already sprinting away off up the road.

There was no sign of Micky Pats when they got to their digs, and when Hennessy inquired as to his whereabouts, his daughter said that he was lying down having a nap.

After lunch Hennessy went out for another swim, leaving Brooks putting together provisions for their excursion with the girls. It was a glorious summer's day, with a clear sky and hardly a ripple stirring the surface of the sliding sea. At one end of the beach a few families with children had taken up residence and their voices came to Hennessy as distant pinpricks in the immensity of the silence that surrounded him far out in the reaches of the bay.

He was just about thinking of going back in when a fair-sized motor boat appeared around a headland and scythed through the water in his direction. He waved to let whoever was in the boat know that he was there and, as it got closer, the engine suddenly died out and the sleek hull eased in beside him. Borne aloft on the billows that overtook the craft's passage, Hennessy saw the familiar face of Seán de Burca looking down at him.

"Come aboard," he shouted, then he leaned down and extended an arm. Hennessy grasped his hand and in a strong grip was pulled over the side, almost losing his bathing trunks in the process.

He sat up and looked about him. The boat appeared to be brand-new, with gleaming pine and chrome fittings, seats with red padded backrests, and a control panel that looked like the console of a spaceship.

"Pretty snazzy, eh?" de Burca said. "Just got it last week."

"You own it? It must've cost you an arm and a leg."

"Yeah, that's why I walk in such a funny way."

de Burca was wearing shorts, a life-jacket and a yachting cap, and he looked every inch the bronzed and carefree sailor.

"You want to go for a trip?" he asked, gesturing at the open sea, and when Hennessy nodded eagerly he handed him a life-jacket, helped him to put it on, then went forward and opened the throttle.

The boat took a leap like a greyhound coming out of the traps and Hennessy went backwards as though pushed by a giant hand. Luckily he ended up in one of the padded seats, otherwise he'd have been splashing in the craft's wake and receding fast.

de Burca made signs of apology and gestured for him to come up beside him and take the wheel. He did so and felt the powerful surge of the boat transmitted up the length of his arms. The bow rose in the air as they cut through the water and the wind of their passage buffeted him so that he had to hold on tight to the wheel. A feeling of elation took hold of him and he shouted, sound without sense, from pure exhilaration.

They went out of the mouth of the bay like a shot from a gun, the waves they made whacking against the sleek sides and bottom of the vessel. Conversation was impossible in the roar of the wind but soon de Burca motioned for Hennessy to move aside and he took the wheel. With practised skill he guided the boat around in a wide curve and took it back in, hugging the shoreline. A currach, manned by two rowers, got caught in the small tidal wave they caused as they passed, and one of the men aboard shook his fist at them.

When they were just off Trá na Reilige, de Burca cut the engine to an idle, took off his yachting cap and ran his fingers through his thick black mane of hair.

"The only way to live," he said. "Speed, danger, standing on the edge and looking over..."

Hennessy, who had come out in goosepimples from the cool sea-breeze, criss-crossed his arms and hugged himself. "It's some boat," he enthused. "It'd be perfect for water-skiing."

"Have you tried it?" de Burca asked, looking interested.

"No, but I wouldn't mind having a go. I suppose you're an expert?"

"That's right. Not much opportunity to compete here but I've tried my hand in England and on the continent."

"I bet you won, too."

de Burca didn't deny the fact. He was obviously a very self-assured character, not in the usual run of teachers that Hennessy had come across. False modesty would not come easy to him; he looked like a man of action, talked like one and by his demeanour behaved like one. There was an air of recklessness about him and maybe even a whiff of danger. A good man to be with in an emergency but also likely to be the one to have caused the emergency in the first place.

Now he uncapped a bottle of beer for himself and a Coke for Hennessy, and they sat and let the sun warm their chilled bodies. The boat rocked gently and a couple of inquisitive seagulls hovered with outstretched wings almost within touching distance.

"You're staying in the Ó Fatharta house," de Burca said, more as a statement than a question.

"That's right."

"Are you not put off by sleeping so close to a graveyard?"

"Funny you should mention that. I woke up during the night and saw a light down there."

"In the graveyard?"

"Yep."

de Burca stretched lazily, then took another swig of beer. "A bit odd, don't you think?"

"Very odd."

"Grave-robbers?"

"Hardly."

"You must have some idea what was going on?"

"I haven't. But why do I get the feeling that you're going to explain it for me?"

de Burca grinned.

"You know, you're a pretty sharp cookie," he said. "Not someone to be underestimated."

"Likewise, I'm sure."

de Burca nodded. Then he took another long, slow draught of beer, the muscles in his arm rippling as he raised the can to his mouth.

"I don't really know what was going on," he said, "but I could hazard a guess. There's a fair bit of money to be picked up from making poteen but, as you probably know, it's illegal. The guards are always on the look-out for stills, so sometimes the locals have to use a bit of ingenuity in hiding them. Now a graveyard is sanctified ground. No one would ever interfere with the dead."

"That's right," Hennessy concurred, his poker face matching his companion's.

"Of course, some of these very dead were great poteen makers when they were alive. Hard to see them objecting if their descendants used their place of rest to carry on the trade..."

Hennessy put his finger along by the side of his nose and nodded his head. "They'd need to get a better night-watchman, though," he said. "One who didn't spend most of his time sampling the goods."

"You mean?"

"Old Micky Pats, Miss Ó Fatharta's father. I found him lying on top of one of the graves this morning as plastered as a broken leg."

"Did you now?"

The boat had been drifting in towards the shore and de Burca had to rev up the engine to take it back out to sea. The noise frightened the gulls and they squawked raucously in protest.

"I'll have to go," Hennessy said. "I'm meeting some friends to take a look round the village."

de Burca nodded. "We'll have to do this again sometime," he said. "I go out most days. And don't worry about the business in the graveyard. I'm only a blow-in myself but I'll pass the word along in the right quarters. A poteen still is usually portable and can easily be moved to another situation. And no need to get anyone upset by mentioning this around. Best to leave a hornet's nest unpoked..."

They stared at one another and, although the sun was quite hot, Hennessy once more felt a chill. In spite of his friendly grin, there was a distinct suspicion of menace in de Burca's attitude. What was that phrase about the iron fist in the velvet glove?

7

*"Oh, we're off to see the wild west show,
The elephants and the kangaroo-oo-oo-o,
Never mind the weather, as long as we're
    together,
We're off to see the wild west show..."*

Arms linked, Hennessy and Brooks, Kitty and Elsie
went skipping and singing down the road that led
out of Tóin le Gaoith. If any of their teachers had
heard them carolling in English, they would have
been for the high jump, but the brilliant sunshine,
the freedom from classes and the prospect of the
long summer afternoon stretching ahead combined
to make them heedless of all strictures.

Miss Ó Fatharta had told them about a coral
strand, the only one of its kind along that coast,
and that was where they were bound. They passed
a house on a hill and two small frenzied dogs
scurried out, yelping threateningly, but their bark
was worse than their bite and they stayed safely
back behind the surrounding fence.

From the brow of the hill the four of them got
a good view of the beach. The land leading down
to it was broken up by stone walls into tiny fields,
and they were mathematically laid out in drills

that boasted flowering potato stalks. A donkey and a black-and-white cow shared a patch of scrub, while a goat with a tinkling bell tied around his neck threw his head up and down as though saying yes, yes, yes.

Further out near the mouth of the bay the sea was choppy but closer in to the shore it was still and calm. Under the glare of the sun the coral strand was startlingly white, water-washed to a newness that hurt the eyes. On the widened parking space above it a number of cars and mini-buses were crowded together in a haphazard fashion, and the grassy slopes below that again were packed with people in various states of undress.

"We'll be lucky to get standing room here," Kitty said critically. "They must've heard we were coming."

Brooks, perspiring profusely, put the knapsack with the provisions in it on the ground, then sat on it. His Hawaiian shirt had wilted in the heat and his face was as red as a beetroot.

"We'll go further on along the coast," Hennessy decided. "Bound to find a spot somewhere."

Brooks, however, refused to budge any further. "I'm not going another inch," he said stubbornly. "My head hurts, my feet are in bits and my underwear's up around my neck."

"I don't wish to know that," Kitty said, wrinkling her nose with distaste. "The thought of your underwear does absolutely nothing at all for me."

"It does very little for me right now either,"

Brooks responded.

After some discussion they came to a compromise. Kitty and Hennessy, who were the more athletic anyway, would go on and explore the coastline and maybe have a swim; Elsie and Brooks would rest up, take in a little sun and perhaps follow on later in the fullness of time.

"Don't scoff all the grub," Hennessy said as a parting shot but Kitty mumbled that she couldn't see herself eating any of it anyway after Brooks sitting on it.

Up near the grass margin the coral was chunky and it crunched noisily under their feet; down near the water, though, it was finer and had a grainy texture like sifted gravel. There were a lot of outcrops of rock, and they made their way along one of these, a ridge that stretched out like a finger pointing into the sea. The water was clear and cold-looking, its depth difficult to judge because of the false perspective.

Hennessy merely had to discard shirt, shorts and sandals to be ready for a swim but for Kitty it appeared to be a more complicated operation.

"You go ahead," she told him. I'll catch up with you."

He did as he was bid, diving deep down into the breath-snapping embrace of the chill Atlantic. As soon as he surfaced he went into a crawl, churning through the water until his body temperature and that of the sea equalised; then he turned on his back and began to float.

He was stretched out in the cruciform position, minding his own business and at peace with the world, when he was suddenly grabbed from underneath and pulled struggling into the bluey-green depths. The first thought that struck him was that Jaws had returned and he was about to be ingested like Jonah into the whale's belly. Then, as his panic subsided, he realised that it was a human form that had hold of him and, as the bubbles cleared, he saw the tight blonde curls and grinning face of the playful Kitty.

They came to the surface together, Hennessy hawking and spitting water and totally outraged. As soon as he got his breath back, he accused her of trying to drown him, of being completely irresponsible and of having no thought of the consequences of her act: "You could've drowned the both of us," he told her. "The fishes plucking out our eyes, eels ferreting up our noses."

"Aaagh." Kitty made a face. "Don't be such an old granny. It was only a bit of fun. You looked so smug, floating there, I just had to ring your bell..."

"Don't worry, I'll get you back."

They were both good swimmers and they raced one another out further into the bay. A seal surfaced a little way from them and watched them with his gleeful, bold child's face. When they made to come closer he dived, splitting the water as effortlessly as a knife slices through butter. Just for a moment his sleek, greyish-blue body could be glimpsed;

then he was gone like a shadow when the sun goes in.

When Hennessy began to feel cold he swam back to the rock and climbed out. He rubbed himself down briskly, laid his towel out on the pitted surface and sat on it. His goosebumps soon disappeared but for a long time he could taste the salt water on his lips.

Kitty came and joined him and they shared the towel. Water glistened in the whorls of her hair, and her shoulder where it touched his was cool but not unpleasant.

"What d'you say we go together for a day or two and see how it works?" she suddenly said, not looking at him but gazing out to sea.

"Go together?"

"You know, be an item. Darby and Joan. Ball'n chain."

"I'd be your boyfriend."

She turned and looked at him. "Nothing heavy, you understand. Not exclusive like...If either of us sees something else we fancy...Well, you know..."

"Seems okay to me."

"That's a bargain then?"

She had her glasses in her hand, but she didn't put them on. After a moment she said, "Seems to me a bargain should be sealed in some manner."

"Cut ourselves and let the blood mix and be blood brothers?"

"Well, not that extreme. Maybe a kiss...?"

She closed her eyes and leaned towards him and

Hennessy quickly brushed her lips with his. To his surprise she stayed as she was, eyes closed, mouth pursed. He tried again and she nestled against him and he could feel her heart beating. About to go for the hat trick, he suddenly noticed that the seal had popped up again and was grinning at him from about a yard away. Hennessy winked at him, then did the necessary one more time.

They stayed where they were until the tide turned and the water began to sidle in over the outcrop of rock. They had to retreat pretty rapidly to avoid getting wet all over again.

There was still no sign of the others, so Hennessy suggested that they do a little more exploring. Kitty readily agreed. To Hennessy the ease of their new status made him feel really good. Up to this his relationship with girls had been that of a fly with a spider's web. He had made tentative advances towards one or two but had always tripped over his own good intentions. Now suddenly he felt like a man of the world, experienced, sophisticated, a real cool dude.

They wandered along in the hot sun, sometimes holding hands, sometimes not. The inlet bit deeply into the land, the shoreline rock strewn and quite often difficult to negotiate. They came to a headland, got around it with much slipping and sliding, then saw a small concrete jetty in front of them.

On a flat stretch of grass overlooking the water, a motorbike and sidecar were parked. Beside them, and leaning drunkenly as though about to topple over, a dirt-stained and much-patched tent had been carelessly pegged. A tiny Irish flag was fixed to the front pole of this tent but it too drooped as though ashamed to be adorning such a shabby fixture.

"I know the guy that owns that machine," Hennessy said, gazing about him.

"He must be down on his luck," Kitty said critically. "That tent is on its last legs."

Hennessy went over and stuck his head inside the flap but, except for a strong odour of old socks, there was no sign of the occupant. A ground sheet was laid out, and there was also a gas primus stove, a soot-stained kettle, a grease-encrusted frying-pan, a chipped cup and saucer and a bottle of sour-looking milk.

"This guy really lives in style," Kitty said, sticking her head in beside his. "Remind me not to accept if he ever invites us for tea."

While Kitty sat on a stone and combed her hair with an implement that looked like a miniature garden fork, Hennessy went over to the edge of the jetty and looked down. The incoming tide was making small waves and a rowing boat moored to an iron stanchion bobbed gently up and down. Stretched out in it, a straw hat shading his eyes and clad in an old-fashioned bathing suit with straps that went over his shoulders, was Jethro Cosgrave. A piece of hairy rope was tied to his big toe, and it went from there over the side of the boat and into the scummy green water that lapped against the stone wall of the jetty.

"Hey," Hennessy called. "Shark on the starboard bow. Your big toe's in danger of being gnawed."

Showing no particular hurry or surprise when he pushed back the hat to reveal his face, Jethro squinted up at Hennessy.

"Aha," he said lazily, "the voice of the turtledove is heard in the land. You're welcome to this neck of the woods, friend of my yesterdays. Pull up a seat and we'll break bread."

Remembering the state of the inside of the tent, Hennessy said hastily, "Afraid we're in a bit of a hurry. Promised to meet up with some people..."

"We? You've a companion with you?"

"Yes, me," Kitty said, suddenly appearing by Hennessy's side. "How's the fishing?"

"Not a bite all day. Must be gone on their holidays." Jethro shook his head, then hauled in the rope and unfastened it from his toe. "So God created the great sea monsters," he said, "and every living creature that moves, with which the waters swarm, according to their kinds...Genesis...And there was evening and there was morning, a fifth day..."

"Some funny friends you've got," Kitty muttered to Hennessy; then out loud she said, "They say the lobster feels nothing when he's dropped into the boiling water, but I don't believe that. What d'you think?"

"I think it takes his breath away."

The rowing boat bobbed crazily when Jethro stood up; but with a surprisingly smooth movement he caught hold of the stanchion and hoisted his great length up and over the edge of the jetty. He leaned there looking at them, the straw hat tipped over one eye, his hand caressing the stubble on his long lantern jaw.

Kitty, who had taken off her glasses, now put them on again. She looked up at Jethro and asked him, "D'you ever get frost on top of your head when you move about?"

He grinned. Then suddenly flipped himself over and stood on his hands. His hat fell off but balancing on one hand he used the other to pick it up and jam it back on his head. From his upside-down position he said, "Now I'm looking up to you. Only problem is, everything is inclined to fall out of your pockets when you walk around like this."

He strutted about a little and then with another graceful movement righted himself. In doing it, his long thin body seemed to float in the air.

"So," Hennessy said, "you're still around. I thought you were heading out to the islands? Looking for a cloud to disappear into..."

"That was the intention, yes, but I got lazy. I pitched my tent and became stuck in meditation. Also my bike's broken down and I'm waiting for a part to be delivered..."

Taking his hat off again and doing a sweeping bow, he sat down cross-legged on the ground.

From a pocket in his old-fashioned swim-suit he produced three lollipops. He gave each of them one, stuck the third in his mouth and talked around it, Kojak-style: "What of your two friends, the musicians? Have they performed to the acclaim of thousands yet?"

"Swift and O'Brien? They'll be lucky if they earn their supper. A tough business to be in, the music business."

"And dangerous? Take drugs, for example, and other mind-blowing substances. Look at what befell old Elvis, Jimi Hendrix, Phil Lynott, Janis Joplin…"

"Janis who?" Kitty asked.

"Janis Joplin, who could belt it out with the best of them. ODed on heroin while still in her prime…"

"I don't think Swiftie and Nedser are in that league," Hennessy said. "It's not that they haven't got their feet on the first rung of the ladder, they can't even find the ladder."

"Still, the drugs are readily available. Are you trying to tell me you've never been offered a whiff or a smoke or a toke…?"

Hennessy and Kitty looked at one another. "What is this?" Kitty asked. "What're you leading up to? Are you a pusher or what?"

Jethro put his hands out, palms upward. "The very opposite," he said. "I strive to warn, not to provide. You see before you a much-reformed individual. Once upon a time I was into drugs and I fell as low as a snake's belly. Then, when I was at my lowest ebb, I had a vision. My grandfather, that good old man, appeared to me in a shower of light—at least, I think it was my grandfather—and counselled me to mend my ways or I'd be damned to everlasting torment. So, hitching myself up by my braces and by the seat of my pants, I forsook the path of evil, took up the Bible and came out of the darkness and into the light..."

Kitty had been staring at him with her mouth open. Now she closed it with an audible snap and said, "Are you winding me up? Are you pulling my chain? What are you, some kind of spaceman?"

She got to her feet and walked away. Then she came back and, including Hennessy in her glare, said, "The two of you are in it, aren't you? It's some kind of set-up. Well I'll tell you something, I don't like to be made fun of. Get yourselves another Patsy—my name's Kitty..."

"Hey, wait a second," Hennessy protested. "You've got this all wrong. I didn't know this guy'd be here or that he'd come out with such a spiel. He's winding me up as much as you..."

His words fell on the empty air, for a determined Kitty was already backtracking the way they had come, the speed of her going giving ample evidence of the intensity of her temper. If there had been any fascinated onlookers they would have seen steam coming out of her ears.

"Now look at what you've done," an angry Hennessy exclaimed to a far from apologetic-looking Jethro. "You've ruined a beautiful friendship before it even had a chance to get off the ground. What'd you have to come out with all that rubbish for?"

"It's not rubbish. Drugs are becoming easier and easier to get, especially by young people. And they may not be as far away from this seemingly green and pleasant place as you think. Mark my words..."

"They've already left their mark."

Jethro shrugged. "Keep your eyes open, just the same," he said. "Sometimes it's from the unlikeliest of situations that danger comes. And beware of false friendship when it is offered, because sometimes it comes clothed in a smiling face cloaking a black heart..."

"Is that another quotation from the Bible?" a still angry Hennessy asked him.

Smiling, Jethro said, "No, I made that up myself. Sometimes even the Bible has to be given a helping hand."

8

"Cripes, she'd some head of steam up," Brooks said, obviously getting a great amount of enjoyment from the telling. "She looked ready to chew nails..."

"I know; I know; you've told me half a dozen times," a red-faced Hennessy replied. "Can't you give it a rest?"

They were walking towards the Ó Fatharta residence, the descending sun streaking the sky crimson behind their backs. A cool breeze had got up, appearing to be even chillier because of their heat-warmed skin.

The remainder of the afternoon had been a disaster. By the time Hennessy had met up with Brooks, the girls had hightailed it for other parts, Kitty dragging a protesting Elsie along with her—she had been protesting, Brooks was at pains to point out, because of having to depart from his presence rather than at having to leave the food and drink behind.

"Fat chance of that," Hennessy had scoffed, a remark that had offended his friend and caused him to keep harping on how angry Kitty had been.

They were still arguing when they turned into the lane leading to the cottage. About halfway down they met Micky Pats, leaning on his stick and winded from his evening walk. In his day he must have been a big man but age had withered the flesh from his bones and his clothes now hung on him like garments draped across a clothes horse to dry. His face had caved in, the absence of teeth causing his chin almost to touch his nose. Like a cow, he was forever chewing the cud, in his case a wad of tobacco whose juice he could unerringly direct to drown whatever unfortunate insect happened to cross his path. It was a virtuoso performance that Brooks especially would have loved to be able to copy.

Now he greeted them in Irish, swaying slightly on his stick as if the alcohol content in his blood was still above the standing-upright limit.

"What'd he say?" Hennessy asked Brooks, unable himself to follow the old man's staccato delivery.

"He said that a red sky at night's a farmer's delight..."

"Well, tell him a red sky in the morning is a sailor's warning."

"He said that too...You didn't let me finish."

"Okay, then ask him which corpse down in the graveyard sells the poteen."

"I can't ask him that."

"Why not?"

"It wouldn't be right. Making fun of an old man..."

"It's not to make fun of him. I really want to know."

"How can a corpse sell anything?"

"Aw, you know what I mean."

"I don't."

"Now you're getting thick..."

"I'm not...And you can get stuffed."

"My, my," Hennessy said, recoiling in mock horror. "Such language, I dunno where you get it from..."

Brooks said something far worse, nodded at Micky Pats, went around him and stumped off towards the house. Hennessy looked at the old man and made a circling sign with his finger against the side of his head to indicate madness. Micky Pats grinned toothlessly, then let fly with a squirt of tobacco juice that just missed Hennessy's left ear and brought to a watery grave a stick fly that had been innocently sitting on a leaf enjoying the evening air.

In the west, the sun gave a technicoloured yawn, pulled the purple-tinted clouds up to its chin, then ducked its head below the horizon.

That evening there was a getting-to-know-you social in the school yard. Teachers mingled with the students, encouraging them to meet and talk but this gave an air of artificiality to the proceedings which, if left to themselves, the guys and girls would have soon shaken off.

Kitty and Elsie at first avoided Hennessy and Brooks like the plague but eventually they got talking and the little disagreement of the afternoon faded quickly into the past.

"He's a weirdo, that Jethro," Hennessy said. "It's hard to know what to make of him. All that quoting from the Bible...And then his story about being hooked on drugs."

"He told us his granda appeared to him in a shower of light," Kitty explained to the others.

Elsie gave one of her usual giggles, then said, "Maybe Scottie beamed him down."

A few guitars had appeared and were being strummed, and they joined a group who were attempting to sing "The Fields of Athenry." As usual, no one knew the words.

"When're your friends making their débuts?" Kitty asked Hennessy during one of the many fumbling pauses.

"Tomorrow night. But the pub is off limits."

"So you won't be able to go?"

"Maybe. Then again maybe I will. Go, that is."

"You'll chance it?"

Hennessy shrugged.

"You'll be skinned alive," Kitty told him seriously. "Sent home in disgrace..."

"Would you miss me?"

"Now you're fishing for compliments."

"I could plead insanity if I'm caught."

"Now that's a thought..."

Just then, Tommy Ugly appeared. He was still wearing the khaki shorts, and an Aran sweater and a cap as big as a dustbin lid completed his outfit. Whatever one might say about him, he was certainly larger than life, the kind of character one heard about but seldom met. Brooks had volunteered the possibility on the way down that Tommy Ugly was really the headmaster of their school in Dublin done up in disguise: "It's amazing what can be done with make-up nowadays," he had said. "And remember the way old Housey was always disappearing. He could've been going off to Tommy Ugly's school to be him..."

Hennessy had pooh-poohed the idea, although at the same time suggesting that Brooks should put his theory to the test by trying to pull the headmaster's beard off.

Now, showing great versatility on the mouth organ, Tommy Ugly, or whoever he was, got a sing-song going in Irish, and soon the lusty strains of "An Poc ar Buile" were battering the night sky. This was followed by a string of other favourites and an hour passed pleasantly for those who were singing, if not for passers-by and those in adjoining houses who had to listen.

When the session finished Hennessy and Brooks walked Kitty and Elsie home, then took a detour on the way back to visit Swift and O'Brien.

They were living in an outhouse-cum-shed at the back of An Súgán, the pub where they were due to perform on the following night. As well as being their lodgings, it also doubled as a store. The sweet-sour smell of alcohol was overpowering and Nedser O'Brien maintained that just breathing the air made him feel tipsy.

The two of them had to sleep on pull-down

beds in the outer room, while a stoutly padlocked door kept them from investigating the pub's stock of intoxicating liquor. There was no electric light and they had to make do with an oil lamp that threw more shadows than a haunted house.

"It's a bit like Dracula's lair," Brooks said, gazing with some trepidation about him. "You haven't seen any bats with six-foot wing-spans, have you?"

"Don't knock it," Swift said. "At least the roof doesn't leak."

"How d'you know? It hasn't rained yet."

They told Hennessy and Brooks about their landlord, Joe Máire: "For starters, he's got a glass eye," O'Brien said. "It just sits there and looks at you. But at least it's better than the other one which rolls around like a mad marble."

"Yeah, he's something to see," Swift agreed. "I think he's made up of leftovers, an arm here, a leg there...And at some stage of his birth he could've fallen into an acid bath: he looks kinda dissolved, you know what I mean?"

"He must be some sight..."

"But not for sore eyes. Remember Lurch from the Addams Family? This guy has to be related to him."

Hennessy had been examining the padlock on the storeroom door, twisting it this way and that. "Give us a loan of your plectrum," he asked O'Brien, and when he was handed the sharp piece of plastic he inserted the point in the lock and fiddled it about.

"You think you can open it?" Swift asked him.

"Who knows? I'm just foolin' around. It'd be interesting to see what's inside."

"Interesting! It'd be bloody marvellous. Free gargle for the boys and a chance to put one over on Joe Máire. Lovely-doubly..."

Brooks, who had been morosely watching Hennessy interfering with the lock, suddenly said, "I think we should stop right now. I've a bad feeling about breaking into that storeroom. I can feel trouble looming as sure as my name's Alfred..."

"Alfred?"

"My *nom de plume*."

"Get out've it."

"Honest. Whenever I write something on a wall I sign it Alfred. You know, like 'Kilroy Was Here.'"

"Come to think of it, I have seen that name scrawled around the school up in Dublin," O'Brien said. He gazed at Brooks with new interest. "You've been hiding your light under a bushel, Brooksie old chum."

Brooks did an Oliver Hardy simper and twiddled an imaginary tie.

"What kinda thing d'you write?" Swift inquired.

"Oh, you know...'Tomorrow is cancelled because of lack of interest,' or 'When the bomb falls place your head between your legs and kiss your ass goodbye.' That sort of thing..."

"Well, you old thistle-stamper..."

"Could you knock off the admiration society for a minute," Hennessy suddenly called. "I think I've got this thing open."

The other three crowded around him, jostling for position.

"Stand back a bit," he ordered, then to Swift: "Bring the lamp over here and give us some light."

With a final wrench he pulled the padlock free. Then he ran the chain through the iron loop embedded in the door. He placed his hand against the rough timber and pushed, and the door creaked inwards with a sound like paper tearing.

"Great balls of fire," Brooks breathed, "this is a bit like *Fright Night II*..."

They pushed their way in, with Swift holding the oil lamp aloft so that the light spilled over a wider area. The room had been carved out of the rock face that the shed backed on to and the air was as cold as the inside of a fridge. Crates were stacked from floor to ceiling, with narrow passage-ways wide enough to admit only one person at a time branching off between them. There was a dank smell of stale beer, and in the gloom they could hear a frenzied scurrying as though small animals had been interrupted at play.

A horrified Brooks exclaimed, "Rats...them's rats..." and prepared to retreat.

The other three paused, stood poised for flight, then Hennessy laughed and said, "Are we chicken or what? Leave old cowardy custard Brooks to keep watch and we'll take a look around. He can give us the nod if he sees anyone coming..."

A relieved Brooks was only too glad to comply,

and he hastily back-pedalled out into the other room. They could hear his voice echoing hollowly as he talked to himself to keep up his courage.

They stood grouped close together and undecided about what to do next. Again it was Hennessy who took the initiative and said, "We'll split up and try a few of these passages. I can feel a breeze, so there must be another opening somewhere. Let's see where it leads..."

"What'll we do for light?" a nervous O'Brien asked.

"We'll put the lamp on top of one of the piles of crates. That should give us enough to see where we're going."

But O'Brien was still reluctant to budge.

"Why don't we just grab a few cans of beer and leave it at that?" he muttered obstinately. "What's the point of wandering around in the dark and maybe being bitten by a rat. They can give you blood poisoning, you know. An uncle of mine got it in his finger and his whole arm swole up and turned purple."

"He got it from a rat?"

"Did he?"

"That's what I'm asking you."

"How do I know? But he must've got it somewhere. Stands to reason..."

"For cryin' out loud!"

An exasperated Hennessy stared inquiringly at Swift. "Are you weak in the pins too?" he asked him. "D'you want to go back out and join 'Nervous-

Knees' Brooks as well?"

In the silence they could hear water dripping, then a rustle as though of wings up near the roof.

"Bats," an appalled O'Brien breathed with certainty.

Their minds made up, and discretion being the better part of valour, the three of them turned tail and scurried back the way they had come, and erupted into the outer room in a rush.

Brooks, when he saw them coming, made a beeline for the door but his huge shadow cast by the lamp still held aloft in Swift's hand caused him to veer away. "What happened, what happened?" he asked, turning to face them. "What'd youse see?"

"Nothing," Hennessy answered, mock calmly. "We just decided to wait for a better time to have a look around. Late at night, maybe, when everyone's in bed."

"Then why'd you come running out as if a herd of ghosts was on your tail?"

"We thought a little exercise was in order."

"You did in your foot. You were trying to put the wind up me."

"And we succeeded, didn't we?"

"As it happens, I was about to go in and get you. Either Joe Máire or Quasimodo is on his way over here. Take a look."

Swift gave a quick glance out the window, then nodded. "That's him," he said. "He must've heard the commotion."

By the time the man in question had stuck his head in the door, however, the four of them were sitting round the rickety table that was one of the room's few pieces of furniture, absorbed in a game of cards. The door to the inner sanctum was closed, the padlock seemingly back in place. Only Brooks' trembling hands as he dealt the cards gave evidence of anything being amiss.

Joe Máire was not quite so ugly as the description furnished by Swift and O'Brien would have led the others to believe. He did have a lazy eye, it was true, with a permanently stuck, half-closed eyelid, and the other one had the mad look of a mechanism that had to do all the work by itself but otherwise his features were reasonably matched. He was a big, bulky man, with a shambling gait and huge knotted arms that swung almost to the ground as he walked. He looked strong enough to pluck up the trunk of a tree and pick his teeth with it.

"What's this?" he growled when he saw the four of them sitting round the table. "Where'd them other two come from? If they're going to stay here they'll hafta pay rent..."

"Just visiting," Hennessy explained. Feeling called upon to say more, he went on, "We're on the Irish course. We're friends of Swift and O'Brien."

"Swift and O'Brien?"

"He knows us as Dave and Ned, the kings of country music," Swift whispered, looking embarrassed.

In the sudden silence, Brooks tittered nervously, causing Joe Máire to glare at him.

"Well, we'd love to stay and chew the fat," Hennessy said, standing up, "but we've really got to be going. Curfew is at ten. Any later than that and we'll be court-martialled and put in the brig..."

"Huh?"

"Nice to have met you."

Dragging Brooks by the arm, Hennessy made for the door, sidled around Joe Máire and stepped outside. The sense of relief they both felt overcame any feelings of remorse at having to leave Swift and O'Brien behind. In some circumstances it is better not to stand upon the order of your going but go at once!

9

That night Hennessy had an uneasy sleep and dreamed of a man-sized bat with Joe Máire's head that kept asking him questions in Irish. When he couldn't answer, the monster spat great gouts of tobacco juice at him which dissolved just before making contact with his head.

It was with a sense of relief that he suddenly awoke, his eyelids snapping open as though made from elastic. Moonlight was streaming into the room giving it a pale luminescence that imparted a silvery sheen to even the most colourless of objects. The only sound that disturbed the silence was once again Brooks' snoring, regular snorts that came and went with the regularity of a metronome.

Hennessy lay as he was for a moment; then quietly he slid out from under the covers and went to the window. He felt as though he were being guided by some unseen force, a strange sensation that caused him to imagine he was gliding rather than walking in the normal manner.

He put his face close to the glass and looked out. Everything seemed as it should be: the path from the back of the house was clearly outlined, the graveyard was merely shadow and substance, the sea a distant glimmer. Then, before his fascinated gaze, a figure abruptly detached itself from the shelter of the crouching angel, stood for a second or two, then disappeared from his view as if swallowed up by the ground.

He stayed at the window for a little while longer but nothing else occurred out of the ordinary. The scene outside appeared so innocent that he began to doubt that he had, in fact, seen anything at all. It could have been a trick of the light, he told himself, an optical illusion. But he knew in his heart that there was someone there and he was equally certain that he would not get back to sleep unless he went out and did a little investigating.

Not on his own, though! In a situation like this, a companion, never mind how reluctant, would be imperative, even if it were only to keep him company while they both turned and ran away.

Resolutely he went across to Brooks, caught him by the shoulder and shook it. The result was highly satisfying. Brooks rose up like a helium-filled balloon, a bleating "Whaaaaa" issuing from him that hit the ceiling and then bounced off the walls. The next thing he did was not quite as satisfying, however, for he proceeded to encircle Hennessy's neck with his hands and squeeze with a drowning man's grip.

"Get off me, you mutt," Hennessy managed to stutter but after that his full attention was taken up in endeavouring to loosen his attacker's clasp before his wind was cut off permanently.

When Brooks saw who it was that he was trying

to strangle, he let go and allowed his hands to fall to his sides.

"What's wrong?" he asked, looking around the room. "What'd you wake me up for?"

"I wanted you to come and run a four-minute mile with me, you great lump. You nearly killed me. A couple more seconds and I'd've been as limp as a week-old mackerel."

"I'm sorry," a far from sorry-looking Brooks said. "I was dreaming I was being chased by Joe Máire brandishing a giant thistle..."

"That's funny, I was dreaming about him too. He certainly made an impression on us."

"Yeah, like a hatchet on a turkey's neck. Is that what you woke me up to tell me?"

"No, I want you to get up and come outside the back with me. I've seen someone down in the graveyard..."

Brooks looked at him in horror. "You just have to be joking..." He folded his arms across his chest to show that he had no intention of moving anywhere.

"Come on, Brooksie, don't be a maiden aunt. As Sherlock Holmes might say, the game's afoot..."

"I don't care if it's an arm and a leg, I'm not budging out of this bed. I'd look lovely traipsing around in a graveyard in the middle of the night in my pyjamas..."

"Aw, for the love of Mike! Where's your sense of adventure? Haven't you got any backbone?"

"I have. And I aim to keep it firmly in place and

not have some musical ghostie using it as the bow
for his fiddle. Now go back to bed and let me do
likewise. Even Joe Máire and his giant thistle'd be
preferable to playing tag with spooks..."

"That's your last word on the matter?"

"Last, final, ultimate, and for ever. Let it be
recorded that Alfred Aloysius Brooks, in the full
possession of his mental powers and with malice
towards none, refuses to get up in the middle of
the night for the purpose of playing 'now you see
me, now you don't' with a collection of weirdies.
So there..."

And on that note, Brooks lay back, pulled the
covers over his head and did his best to become
invisible.

Hennessy remained staring at the lump in the
bed, then he sighed and went over and began
pulling trousers and sweater on over his pyjamas.
He thought about a torch, decided the moon
would afford enough light, pulled up the window
and wriggled his way through.

The night was indeed still and chill and things
that in daylight looked ordinary and commonplace
now took on strange and even threatening shapes.
A branch of a tree appeared raised as if to strike,
an upturned wheelbarrow was a crouching animal
ready to pounce, the turf stack might have been
a door into another dimension. Not for the first
time, Hennessy cursed the possession of an over-
active imagination, willing it to go back to sleep
like Brooks and let him get on with his furtive

journey.

He was wrong about Brooks, though. Just about to step over the stile that led into the graveyard he suddenly felt a touch on his shoulder that petrified him into immobility. Then a familiar voice whispered in his ear, "Hey, all for one and one for all. You didn't really think I'd let you down, did you?"

He turned, to see Brooks' platter face peering over his shoulder, another moon to rival the one in the sky.

Although in reality happy to see him, Hennessy still felt called upon to offer a rebuke: "You frightened the living daylights outta me," he told him. "You're lucky I didn't decapitate you with my famous Banzai karate chop..."

"Is that anything like a lamb chop?"

"Well, instead of you eating it, it eats you."

"What'll they think of next?" Brooks said, shaking his head in admiration.

"Come on, you Cossack's armpit," Hennessy told him. "While we're spending our time talking, the birds'll have flown."

"With a bit of luck..."

Cautiously they stepped it out between the tombstones, one behind the other like participants in a game of Blind Man's Buff. In the moonlight the angel threw a huge shadow, a pool of darkness into which they moved with extreme care. Unsure of his footing, Hennessy put his hand on the stone flank and immediately, as though he had caused it, the ground trembled beneath their feet. It was only a slight tremor but it was enough to make Brooks moan in fright.

"You felt it?" Hennessy asked him in a whisper.

"Felt it! It ran up my leg and bit my bottom. I'm just after aging five years in the space of five seconds..."

"Keep your voice down. They'll hear us..."

"Who'll hear us?"

"Whoever caused that rumble."

Brooks caught Hennessy by the arm. "You know," he whispered conspiratorially, "all my ancestors were champion farters. Maybe that was one of them sending me a greeting..."

"I wouldn't be surprised if it was you yourself. I've heard you in action remember."

Brooks shook his head ruefully. "In all modesty, I have to admit that that one was way out of my league."

Crouching down, Hennessy put his head around the side of the angel, and quickly drew it back again.

"D'you see anything?"

Hennessy pondered, then he said, "I think the noise was caused by the gate of the tomb being either opened or closed. Seán de Burca mentioned that there could be poteen makers about. They might have the stuff hidden in the crypt."

"So? You're not thinking of going down to have a look, are you?"

"Nah, it's none of our business. They're breaking

the law, I suppose, but I'm no stool-pigeon."

"Me neither. Let's get outta here."

They were about to take off when a movement above them caught their attention and arrested their progress. Before their horrified gaze they saw a figure silhouetted against the sky, standing on the bent back of the angel. Tall and wearing a flat hat, it appeared to be covered from head to toe in some kind of long flowing garment. As they watched, the glow of a cigarette or small cigar in the corner of the mouth illuminated a stubbled jaw, and under the brim of the hat could just be discerned the steely glint of half-closed eyes.

"Holy mother of Moses," Brooks breathed, "it's Clint Eastwood."

10

A rag of cloud eased itself across in front of the moon and for about ten seconds darkness imposed itself upon the face of the earth. When the light shone out bright and clear again the figure on the back of the angel had disappeared. There was no sound, no thump of feet, no wind of passage: it really was a case of 'now you see him, now you don't,' a magician's wand being waved, the switching off of the image by some unseen hand.

"Tell me I wasn't seeing things," Brooks begged, down on his knees now in the long grass like a supplicant.

"If so, we both were," Hennessy murmured, "because I saw him too."

"Clint Eastwood?"

"No, although it looked a bit like him."

"Then who was it?"

"Can't you guess?"

"Paddy McGinty's goat?"

"It was Jethro Cosgrave."

"Are you sure?"

"As sure as I am that you're in the process of tearing my trousers off."

"Oh, sorry..."

Brooks let go his grip of Hennessy's nether

garment and pulled himself to his feet. He swallowed hard.

"I think it's time for us to retire gracefully," he said. "I've had enough shocks for one night. As a matter of fact I'm feeling decidedly faint..."

"No, wait a minute," Hennessy held up his hand like a policeman on point duty. "Don't you see? This changes everything. Cosgrave is not a native of this place, no more than ourselves. He wouldn't have anything to do with poteen making. There must be something else going on..."

"Maybe Cosgrave is the Wolf Man and he's come out to bay at the moon?"

"Can't you be serious for a minute?"

"I am being serious. Funny things happen when the moon is full."

"Such as?"

"Witchcraft," Brooks whispered mysteriously. He put his face close to Hennessy's and went on in a deep, sepulchral voice, "The followers of black magic take their clothes off and dance around gravestones. Sometimes they sacrifice a virgin or two..."

"We'd be so lucky."

"Don't scoff, it goes on all the time."

"Says who?"

"Well..." Brooks waved his arm about vaguely. "I read it somewhere."

Hennessy snorted. "You're talking through your left elbow," he told the bug-eyed Brooks. "There's something odd going on all right, but I don't think it's anything to do with witches and warlocks. And I aim to find out what it is, with or without your help."

So saying, he went around the side of the stone monument and disappeared from view.

When Brooks finally plucked up the courage to follow him he found him poking at the lock of the steel grill with a length of bent wire. "Where'd you get that wire?" he asked him.

"Well, it just so happens that, like the Boy Scouts, I came prepared. There's a lesson in that for you somewhere."

"Hah." Brooks sat down on his hunkers and watched his friend twist and turn the tool in his hand. "You'll never get it open," he told him. "You'd need a real professional to unlock that."

"D'you want to have a try?"

"No, sirree...I'm happy enough to sit here with my bum in two halves and wait for myself to freeze and become as rock solid as that angel up there. Who needs a warm bed or eight hours' sleep...?"

With a harsh grating sound, Hennessy suddenly swung the gate open. "See?" he said. "That's what caused the noise we heard. People've been going in and out of here a lot lately."

"Well, here's one who's no intention of following suit."

"Please yourself."

Taking a deep breath, Hennessy slowly shuffled down the stone steps, his hand stretched out in front of him like a sleepwalker. As he descended, the darkness rose up about him like inky water and soon he was lost to view.

Brooks stood up and looked around him, not sure what to do. Ideally he would have liked to do a runner: back up the path, in through the window, to finish with a belly flop into his bed. But he felt he'd be letting Hennessy down if he did that. He could stay and keep guard and wait for him to return—but what if he didn't come back? How would he explain such a disappearance to Molly and Pop Caskey, Hennessy's grandparents? And more importantly, how would he feel himself if something horrible happened to his friend? Not as bad as I'd feel if it happened to me, he consoled himself.

He cocked his ear once more to the little rustlings and murmurings that abounded in the graveyard, and his eyes rounded as he fancied he could hear footsteps directly behind him. Afraid to look around, he stood petrified and inwardly trembling. Were they getting closer? O Lord, yes they were...

With a hop, a skip and a jump he was down the steps and out of the moonlight, his legs moving fast, his feet following, the first nuclear-powered human being in history.

The ground, when it levelled off, was rough and pitted with stones, and this gradually slowed his progress. And, like a theorem by Euclid, the darkness was impenetrable. He blundered along; then suddenly emerged into a much wider space which contained gleamings of light. In the middle of the floor, on a raised dais, stood a stone...was it a coffin? It looked like one. On fear-light feet he tiptoed across towards it, drawn on by a force outside his control.

He was only a couple of paces from the object when there was movement behind it. Some spiky red hair appeared, then a forehead and a pair of eyes...

"Ah Janey Mack..." Brooks gasped. Hurriedly he crossed himself. "I thought it was the Prince of Darkness coming out for his evening blood transfusion."

Hennessy, for it was indeed he, stood up from his crouching position and leaned his elbows on the lid of the stone coffin.

"That's the second time tonight you've crept up on me," he said accusingly. "Why can't you stay with me and save both of us a lot of trouble?"

"Why didn't we stay in our beds in the first place and then there wouldn't've been any problem at all?"

"Well, we're here now and we might as well make the best of it. Come over here till I show you something."

Obedient this time, Brooks went in the direction indicated. The glimmer of light was coming from a hole in the roof of the cavern and when Brooks looked up he could see a slice of moon. Directly underneath this opening squatted a crazy-looking contraption made from what seemed like old galvanized buckets and weirdly bent metal piping. There was an odd smell from it like the fetid odour of rotting vegetation.

"I presume this is a still for making poteen?" Hennessy said, wrinkling his nose.

"Looks like it."

"de Burca must've been right then. We've stumbled on an illicit liquor-making operation."

"Signs on it. Are you satisfied? Can we go back now? I can hear my bed calling me: it's saying, 'Brooksie, Brooksie, where are you at all, at all?'"

"That's typical," Hennessy said, with mock disgust. "We're probably standing on the verge of unravelling some great mystery and all you can think about is your bed. You sound like a big girl..."

"Okay, that's it," Brooks said, suddenly huffed. "This time I am going back. I'm outta here as sure as ducks have webbed feet. So put that in your pipe and smoke it."

Hennessy shrugged, then inclined his head into a listening attitude.

"Did you hear something?"

Brooks stiffened.

"What, what?"

"It seems to be coming from the coffin. A kind of grating sound as if the lid was being shifted."

"The lid?"

"Yes, the lid. It sounds as if there's something inside trying to get out."

Unnoticed by Brooks, Hennessy gave one of the

metal containers that made up the still a resounding
kick. The sound, magnified by the cavern, echoed
from wall to wall.

Brooks let out a squeak as though something
had become stuck in his throat. Wide-eyed, he
gazed back over his shoulder at the stone casket.
Then his legs came to life and he was waddling
rapidly towards the opening that had brought
them there.

"Not that way...Over here..."

Hennessy's shouted command caused him to
veer off at a tangent, then the two of them were
scampering over the uneven ground towards
another exit from the cave. They went through
this and into a narrow passageway that was in
complete darkness but they had only blundered a
short distance into it when Brooks suddenly skidded
to a halt.

"What's wrong now?" Hennessy asked, also
stopping.

"What's wrong? You ask me what's wrong.
We're going in the opposite direction to the way
we came, that's what's wrong. You've tricked me..."

"I didn't. If we'd gone the other way we'd've
had to pass the coffin. I distinctly saw long tentacle
things pushing out of it. Supposing one of them'd
wrapped itself round your ankle...?"

"I'd wrap my fist around your nose if I could
find it."

"Your fist?"

"No, your nose."

"There's gratitude for you."

Their eyes were gradually becoming used to the dark but the narrowness of the passage was still rather frightening. Brooks put out his hand, then quickly drew it back again when he felt the dampness of the wall. "There was nothing in that coffin," he said sullenly. "You just made it up about the noise."

"D'you want to go back then and have a look?"

"What else can we do? I could get stuck in here. I could be buried alive."

"Well, you stay here and I'll go on a bit and see what I can find. I'm sure there's another way out."

"Not on your nanny. I don't want to be here on my own. I'm going with you."

"Right then, follow the whites of my eyes."

"How can I follow the whites of your eyes if I'm looking at the back of your head?"

"I'll walk backways."

"I hope you trip over yourself."

They continued on, and the passage grew wider the further they progressed. Suddenly Hennessy stopped dead once more, Brooks blundering into him.

"What's wrong now?"

"We're there."

"Where?"

There was the rasp of a match and Hennessy was illuminated, holding the tiny flame above his head.

"You louse," Brooks gasped. "You had matches all the time..."

"I had one match, which I had to keep for an emergency. That's all..."

Brooks looked about him, taking in rows of stacked crates, the glint of bottles and the nostril-gripping odour of stale beer.

"Do you recognise where you are?" Hennessy asked him.

In awe, Brooks said, "It's the cave at the back of Swift and O'Brien's kip. We've come in the back door. Can you imagine that...?"

11

Nedser O'Brien was not a happy young man. City-born and -bred, he was never at ease when he had to leave the concrete canyons of Dublin for the more grassy slopes and wide open spaces of the countryside. He had been thirteen before he had seen a cow in its natural environment—i.e. in a field—and a journey out to Bray in the Dart had been the height of his wanderings before this present trip.

Now, as he lay tossing and turning on the narrow camp bed in the shed behind Joe Máire's pub, listening to the shifts, creaks and rustlings common to the great outdoors, he was feeling decidedly uncomfortable. This was a different set of noises to the ones he was accustomed to; lying abed in the city he was used to hearing the clatter of footsteps on concrete pathways, the often ungentlemanly shouts of homeward-bound drunks, the rush and sway of traffic.

But as he looked once more at the illuminated dial of his wristwatch—it was five minutes to twelve—and tried for the umpteenth time to impose his will on the bone-hard bed, he wished fervently for the rumble of a double-decker bus to come and blot out the screams of demented cats and the howling of crazed dogs that were ripping the night apart outside.

Swift, of course, had dropped off as soon as his head hit the pillow. Not even a goodnight out of him. And naturally, as soon as he, O'Brien, had made up his mind to leave the light on, the rotten lamp, to spite him, had guttered, sent up an oily plume of smoke and gone out. The advent of darkness had been as sudden as a plunge over a cliff and for an uneasy moment O'Brien wondered if he had gone blind.

With a frustrated sigh he wriggled over onto his face, then just as quickly flipped himself onto his back again. He put his hands behind his head, gritted his teeth and willed sleep to come and overpower him. It was useless, he might as well resign himself to lying awake all night.

He was staring into the darkness which, under his concentrated gaze, was beginning to press down on him as if it possessed weight, when he fancied that a voice had suddenly come out of nowhere to instruct him to "Beware, for you know not the day nor the hour..."

Holding his breath, he cocked his head and listened carefully and, yes, there it was again. This time it remarked that "Big Brother is watching you. Even your thoughts are being scanned. So clean up your act..."

Horrified, O'Brien felt his face freeze into a grimace of fright. Unable to decide where the disembodied voice was coming from, he came to the conclusion that it might even be issuing from under the very bed he was lying on.

When he could unclench his teeth sufficiently to speak, he whispered, "Hey, Swiftie, is that you? Because if it is, you're scaring the mush outta me. Put a sock in it, will you...?"

There was a pause like an intake of breath, then the voice came again, this time seeming to slither across the floor: "Woe to the unbelievers. You have been warned. If you don't mend your ways, you'll be dipped into a vat of boiling castor-oil..."—the words, broken off, were followed by what sounded suspiciously like a very human giggle.

O'Brien sat bolt upright in bed. He recognised that imitation of a laugh, that excruciating hee-haw like a donkey backfiring. It could belong to only one person: "Brooks, I'll be dug outta you," he yelled, outrage causing his voice to reverberate round the room and surprise even himself.

There was a sudden flurry of activity, then the flare of a match and he could see Swift fumbling to light the stub of a candle that he had earlier anchored into the neck of a bottle placed beside his bed.

"What're you on about?" Swift asked him, the pale candle-flame accentuating the whiteness of his features. His hair was standing on end in spiky points.

"Brooks is in here somewhere," O'Brien explained. "He seems to think it's funny to creep in and put the wind up us with funny voices."

"Where is he?"

They both looked around but in the cramped space of the room there was practically nowhere to hide.

"I could've sworn he was in here," O'Brien faltered. "Maybe he's under the bed."

"Did you look?"

"Where?"

"Under the bed, you jackass."

"I don't think he'd fit."

Nevertheless, O'Brien leaned out and swept his arm around in the narrow space under him. There was a clink and an empty Coke bottle popped out and rolled towards the wall.

"Maybe he's turned into a genie and is in the bottle?"

"No need to be so sarky," O'Brien said, in a hurt tone. "I know what I heard."

They sat and listened, and again the voice whispered at them: "Dave and Ned, your time has come. Prepare to meet your maker, the mad molecule..." Swift flinched, while O'Brien buried his head under the blankets.

Muttering a four-letter word, followed by the second person singular, Swift then went into action. He jumped out of bed and began marching around the room, both fists held aloft. "Come out, wherever you are," he challenged. "Come out and let me have just one swing at you."

"Don't trifle with the spirits of the undead," the voice warned.

"Spirits of the undead my backside...Show yourself, you great fat fool."

"Take it easy, Swiftie," another voice broke in. "Calm down or you'll blow a gasket."

"Hennessy? Is that you? I should've known the pair of you'd be in it. Where are you?"

"We're in the storeroom at the back. Any chance you'd open the door and let us out?"

O'Brien's head had reappeared from under the blankets and he watched as Swift went over to the wooden door at the rear and put his ear to it. The wavering flame from the candle made his crouched figure look misshapen and grotesque.

"How'd you get in there?" he asked, speaking to the door.

"There's a passageway that leads from the graveyard behind our digs. Open up and we'll tell you all."

Swift stood back and surveyed the large padlock on the door. "I'm not an expert at lock-picking like you," he said. "I don't know if I'll be able to manage it."

"It's not closed," Hennessy's voice told him. "I didn't have time to click it into place when Joe Máire appeared on the scene. Just pull it, say 'Open Sesame' and Bob's your uncle..."

"I know what I'd like to pull..."

Grimly Swift took hold of the padlock, gave it a good twist and, sure enough, it came apart in his hand. He pushed the door and it swung inwards to reveal the two interlopers standing grinning at him.

"Leonardo and Raphael, the ninja turtles, at your service," Hennessy said. He extended his hand. "Put it there."

"Certainly I will," Swift said, and he tipped the candle he was holding so that a drip of hot wax fell neatly into Hennessy's outstretched palm. As he let out a roar and started dancing round the room, Swift said to him, "Let that be a lesson to you. Mess around with Dave and Ned and all you'll get is pain, pain, pain...And as for you," he went on, turning to Brooks...

But "Spare me, oh master," was the immediate entreaty there and he was granted the sight of the corpulent Brooks sinking to his knees and raising his hands in supplication.

O'Brien had been watching with much satisfaction the antics of Hennessy as he danced around the room. Now he said, "Aw, shut your cakehole, it serves you right for the fright you gave us. Waking us up in the middle of the night like that..."

Hennessy paused and started blowing on his hand. His eyes were watering and his face was as red as his hair. He threw O'Brien a look that missed him by inches and made a dent in the wall.

"How's about my burning a hole in your other hand?" Swift offered. "Then you could claim the...what d'you call it...?"

"Stigmata," Brooks supplied.

"That's it. People'd be coming to get your

blessing. You'd be more famous than a moving statue."

"If it's all the same to you, I think I'll pass on that one," said Hennessy.

Swift put the bottle with the candle in it on the table, then fished out the butt of a cigarette and lit it from the flame. To Hennessy's disappointment he failed to ignite his nose. Taking a deep drag, he pursed his mouth and expelled a fat and wobbling smoke ring.

While Hennessy continued to haw on his scorched hand, Brooks gave the other two an account of their adventures, telling them how they had seen Jethro Cosgrave in the graveyard, how he'd disappeared and how they'd found the passage that led to Joe Máire's storeroom.

"He didn't come through here," O'Brien said. "I haven't slept a wink. I'd've seen him..."

"There's a warren of passages back there," Hennessy said. "He could've ducked into any of them. What I'd like to know is, what's going on?"

"It's obvious, isn't it?" Swift said. "It's like that teacher, de Burca, told you. Someone is making poteen and Joe Máire's selling it."

"Yeah, I know that. But how come Cosgrave's involved?"

"Why shouldn't he be? He's probably buying it."

"Are you joking? He hasn't a tosser..."

"It's a disguise."

"Naw, I don't go for that."

"Then what d'you go for?"

Absentmindedly Hennessy put his hand on the table but he very quickly took it away again when he saw the wax dribbling down the side of the candle. Once bitten, twice shy. "I think there's something more serious going on," he said. "I feel it in my bones."

"You mean you'd like to feel it in your bones?" Swift sneered. "You've seen too many episodes of the *A-Team*. Cosgrave is a scumbag. Look at the way he dresses, listen to that old Bible rubbish he spouts. You're worse to be taken in by him. And you both talk through your hats..."

"What hat?"

"I was speaking...ah..."

"Metaphorically?"

"See, you're a know-all. Why don't you get on your bike and pedal outta here? And take that onion bag with you..."

"Are you referring to me?" Brooks asked. "I'll have you know..."

"Leave it out, Brooksie," Hennessy interrupted. "Can't you see Swiftie's throwing the head. He and Nedser need their beauty sleep. We'd better leave before we're thrown out."

They moved towards the door in a silence you could cut with a knife.

O'Brien, however, oblivious to any aggro, suddenly called, "Hey, will we see you at the session? A friendly face'd be welcome..."

"Not too many friendly faces around here,"

Hennessy said, glancing at Swift. He paused at the door. "But we'll do our best to be there. That is if I'm not in hospital having my hand de-waxed."

Suddenly grinning, Swift stubbed out the butt of his cigarette on the table. He said, "I know a joke about de-waxing. You want to hear it? It seems this tourist guy in Japan..."

12

When class finished the following day, Hennessy and Brooks hung around until the rest of the students had filed out. Seán de Burca, in an open-necked shirt and immaculate white cotton trousers, was gathering up the textbooks that he had distributed earlier. He had the graceful movements of the born athlete, quick and using a minimum of effort.

"Something I can do for you?" he asked them in Irish, when he saw them loitering by the open door.

They looked at each other, then Hennessy said, "Well, there's something we'd like to discuss with you, but we haven't the Irish to explain it properly. We thought maybe you'd make an exception just for once."

de Burca raised his eyebrows. "You know I can't do that," he said, still in the native tongue. "Even as it is I should put you on report for breaking into English."

Hennessy shrugged and turned to Brooks for help but after a few faltering sentences he too gave up. They looked so down in the mouth that de Burca laughed and said, "Okay, we'll talk about it. But not here. Wait for me outside and we'll take a spin down to the coral strand."

It was another glorious day, the sun fierce on their faces as they leaned against the teacher's car. It was a gun-metal 1991 Saab, with smoked-glass windows and automatic gear shift, a powerful piece of machinery capable of getting up to sixty miles per hour in a matter of seconds. On the first day the students had clustered round it in admiring groups but de Burca treated it as nonchalantly as if it were an old crock that he'd picked up on the cheap from a back-street second-hand dealer.

Now, as he came out and slid in behind the wheel, he looked as assured and confident as a man with not a care in the world. He took a pair of mirror sunglasses out of the glove compartment and put them on, turned the key in the ignition, signalled to the waiting duo to get in—Hennessy in the front passenger seat, Brooks in solitary comfort in the back—and they took off to a shower of envious glances from both teaching staff and pupils.

The well-sprung car glided smoothly over the badly paved road, a slight purr the only sign that it contained a combustion engine at all. Even the rather flea-bitten sheepdog at the crossroads, whose habit it was to chase gleefully after each and every moving vehicle, seemed overawed by the car's grandeur and merely cocked an inquisitive eyebrow as it went by.

They arrived at the coral strand, de Burca parked and they got out and stretched their legs. The beach was deserted at this time of day, the ivory-coloured coral clean and undisturbed. The tide was out and a ring of greenish-yellow seaweed girdled the nearer-in rocks. Out further there was a slight swell and a pair of basking seals—probably Hennessy's friend of the day before bringing along his cousin in the hope of seeing some more action—were rising and falling to the slow motion of the waves.

The three of them sat down on a low stone wall and de Burca broke the silence: "What's this all about then? Problems with the course? Not happy with your digs? Attacked by man-eating bugs? Lay it on me..."

The night before, Hennessy had talked over what they had seen with Brooks and they had agreed that they should mention it to someone. de Burca was the obvious choice but now that the moment had come to tell him, Hennessy was strangely disinclined to be the one to do so. Therefore he sat back and let Brooks launch into the story, and he did so, telling of seeing Cosgrave, of finding the entrance to the crypt and of following the passage until it led to Joe Máire's storehouse.

Somehow in the bright light of day the account lost a lot of its mystery; it sounded like a harmless enough excursion, with Cosgrave's presence in the cemetery open to a number of explanations. After all, Hennessy's own grandfather, Pop Caskey, spent most of the warm days of spring and summer up in Glasnevin graveyard listening to the birds and meditating on this, that and the other. Maybe Jethro, with his religious mania, was of a like-minded turn of thought.

de Burca, however, seemed quite interested in what he had been told. First he whistled through his teeth, then he began to question them closely on various details, with particular attention to where, when and how they had come across Cosgrave.

"You must've seen him around," Hennessy insisted. "He rides a motorbike with a sidecar. He's about seven feet tall, wears a long waxed coat and looks as if he hasn't had a bath since Christmas."

"Yes, now that you mention it, I have seen him around," de Burca said, nodding his head. "And I've wondered about him. But people like him usually travel around in packs..."

"Like Hell's Angels, you mean?" Brooks asked, his eyes popping.

"Something like that."

"Maybe he's the leader and he's come to scout the place out. The rest of them might even be roaring into town right now..." Brooks gave a shiver of anticipation.

"You don't really believe that, do you?" Hennessy asked with a snort. "That's only for the birds. Cosgrave is an off-the-waller. He's not the leader of the gang."

"No, it's probably like I told you at the beginning," de Burca conceded. "Poteen makers in the cemetery and your friend just snooping around trying to see what he can lift. I wouldn't worry about it, if I were you. Where'd you say his tent is pitched?"

Hennessy described the small cement jetty and its location, de Burca listening intently.

"Maybe I'll drop a word in the local garda sergeant's ear," the teacher said. "It'll do no harm for them to keep an eye on him. There's been a few break-ins recently and he'd be a likely customer."

Hennessy, who at heart had a sneaking regard for the bold Jethro Cosgrave, was beginning to feel sorry that he had carried the business this far. He didn't really believe that Jethro was a thief: an odd bod certainly but a thief, no. Still, like Macbeth, he had waded into the gore now too far to pull out but at least he could warn the motorbike warrior off in case he really did intend pulling some stunt or other. He made up his mind to call on him at the earliest available opportunity: a word to the wise might prevent unpleasantness later.

That afternoon a group of students from the course walked around the coast on an ecological trip to view the pollution of the beaches. As usual, what they found was man-made: rubbish discarded by careless holidaymakers, in spite of the fact that a plentiful supply of litter bins was provided; tar, still tacky, near the shoreline; a scum of sewage at one particularly scenic point, floating as a long indecency out into the inlet; and gaping holes at the furthest reaches of the coral strand where illegal gravel-gatherers had excavated.

Tommy Ugly himself was the leader of the expedition, and the more pollution they found, the more angry he became. By the time they had got back to the starting place he was in a state of turmoil that bordered on the maniacal, his eyes rolling in his head, his nose quivering, his beard bristling, even his wellingtons curled up at the toes as though cringing from the garbage they had to wade through.

Gathering the tired and sunburnt students round him, he let off one of his familiar barrages of Gaelic, and it was so guttural and impassioned that those in his immediate vicinity, and even some further back, were drenched by the fall-out. Brooks was one of them and, when the headmaster finally desisted and stumped off to nurse his rage at home, he had to go down to the water and immerse his torso in it to clear away the splatter.

"They say cuckoo-spit is good for warts," Hennessy told him as he rose dripping from the sea. "I wonder what Tommy Ugly's spit is good for?"

"Good for making me go and stand at the back of the crowd from now on," Brooks grumbled. He paused and shaded his eyes. "Who's that talking to Kitty?" he asked. "Look, over there beside that beached boat..."

"Currach."

"What?"

"It's not a boat, it's a currach. Dates back to the year of dot. They were going out fishing in those when they still wore animal skins and picked their teeth with whale bones."

"Not too many people know that...But you still haven't answered my question."

"What question is that?"

"You know bloomin' well what question."

"I think his name's Humphrey," Hennessy said gloomily. "Remember the first day? He was the one that laughed when Tommy Ugly was hitting on you...You could even say he saved your bacon."

"Not intentionally though. I hear he's a bit of a mé féiner..."

"A what?"

"He looks out for himself and it's a straight finger to the rest of us. He's not liked..."

"Kitty seems to like him."

"Are you jealous?"

"No, I'm only green like this because I've turned into Mr Spock. Anyway, how're you getting on with Elsie? Have you both managed to eat your way through your case yet?"

"She's a big eater alright," Brooks acknowledged, sitting down beside Hennessy. "I thought no one could outdo me, but you live and learn. Still, she's a giggle. Always in good form."

Hennessy nodded. He cupped his chin in the palm of his hand and stared at where Kitty was standing talking to the tall blond student. "I'm haunted by guys like that," he said. "Just because I'm short and they're tall. Whenever I hit it off with some girl one of them always comes along to steal her away. What is it about me? Am I jinxed or what?"

"Looks like it," Brooks said, showing no sympathy. He took a deep breath, trying to pull in his massive stomach. "What d'you think?" he asked. "Should I enter for the Mr Universe contest?"

Hennessy looked at him. "You could try wearing a corset..."

"Don't be like that."

Humphrey was still engaging Kitty in earnest conversation and, obviously at something he said, she suddenly let out a loud laugh that flew on the breeze like a poisoned dart in Hennessy's direction. He contrived to scowl and groan at the same time.

Brooks, now vigorously towelling himself, paused and gazed at his friend. "Why don't you go over there and take a swing at him?" he asked. "You've nothing to lose. If you connect and he falls down, then he won't come around her again because he'll know you mean business. On the other hand, if he knocks you down, then he'll be a bully in her eyes for hitting someone smaller than himself. It'd be worth a black eye or a bloody nose."

"It's my eye and my nose."

"You think I wouldn't tackle him if he was chatting up Elsie?"

"I don't think it, I know it. You'd go around cluck, cluck, clucking like a chicken with an egg that backed up instead of going in the opposite direction."

"That's not true. Heavy people can be very light on their feet, you know."

"Yeah, when they're running away."

By this time Brooks had finished drying himself off and was engaged in trying to get his head through the neck of yet another of his brilliantly hued Hawaiian shirts. When his fat red face eventually emerged, it wore the look of someone who'd fought a losing bout with an octopus.

"You'd manage better if you opened the buttons," Hennessy told him. "Some day you'll suffocate yourself. I can just see the headline: 'Youth Strangled by His Own Shirt.'"

"If I opened them I'd have to do them up again. This way I'm economising on labour. It's the same thing as putting on your shoes fully laced or leaving the knot in your tie and pulling it on over your head. No flies on me..."

Hennessy stood up and stretched. People were straggling up the beach, homeward bound, while on a rock at which the incoming tide lapped a boy and a girl stood caught and arrested in motion. Evening always seemed to bring a certain sadness, Hennessy thought, as though it were mourning the close of yet another day. He could feel it, for all the world like a sigh that suddenly takes one by surprise or a note of music that brings back memories of a time in the past.

Shivering the feeling off, he put an arm around

a surprised Brooks' neck. "Let's hit the road, Jack," he told him. "We'll leave Humphrey for another day…"

13

"You're stark, raving nuts, you know," Brooks proclaimed, "but as usual I might as well be talking to the wall."

He was, in fact, talking to a rather odd character who was standing by Hennessy's bed. This gent was wearing a beret pulled down over his ears, the lower half of his face was stained with a substance like soot—it was soot—and the rest of him was enclosed in a large shapeless raincoat, the hem of which touched the floor.

Speaking with Hennessy's voice, this apparition asked plaintively, "You don't think it's a good disguise? Come on, I want the truth. Be honest now..."

"I've been honest for the past half-hour," an exasperated Brooks answered. "If you go out got up like that you'll be arrested before you get to the end of the road. You might as well parade about half naked: you'd draw as much attention to yourself."

"Aw, you're exaggerating. I think it's pretty nifty..."

Not without difficulty—he was standing on the end of the coat—Hennessy got up and looked at himself in the mirror of the wardrobe. "I could be a French midget," he ventured tentatively, pulling the beret down further over his right eye. "Especially if I keep out of the full light. Music places are usually badly lit. I'll stand in the shadows."

"That'll make you look even more suspicious. Why don't you just go as you are and take a chance on not being caught?"

"Cripes, if I'm sent home my grandmother'll do for me. I can't risk that."

"Then why don't you just forget the whole thing? Swiftie and Nedser probably won't even notice that you're not there."

"But I'll notice. A promise is a promise."

"Well, I wash my hands of it..."

Brooks went back over to his open suitcase and took out a number of chocolate bars of different types. He laid them on the bed, then stood back to survey them.

"Laying in provisions for the night?" Hennessy asked him.

"I'm meeting Elsie at the céilí," Brooks said grandly, "and I want to be sure I've enough filler for the intervals."

"If you eat all those you'll throw up on the floor."

"I've no intention of being out on the floor. I'm only going to stand and stare..."

"I thought you said you were light on your feet?"

"When the occasion demands..."

"Hah."

Still gazing into the mirror, Hennessy removed some of the soot from his chin and used it to give himself a moustache. Flexing his knees, he did a funny walk round the room. "You ain't seen nothing yet, kid," he told a bemused Brooks.

"I've seen enough. I'm off."

"I'll go down the road with you."

"Oh, no you won't..."

"Oh, yes I will..."

They exited through the back door, both of them vying to be first out. Hennessy had to keep his hands in his pockets to drag up the coat and avoid tripping over the tail. Walking like that he had a hump on his back and no neck. Anyone seeing him would imagine that he was a leftover from the invasion of the crab men!

"What'll I tell Kitty if she asks where you are?" Brooks inquired. "That is if Humphrey hasn't pegged her for every dance."

"Tell her I've gone on a mission of mercy. Tell her it's a matter of life and death. Tell her I'm balanced on a knife-edge..."

"I'll tell her you've gone down to the pub disguised as a chimney sweep in a flasher's raincoat. That's about the height of it..."

"You wouldn't, would you?"

"Oh, yes I would."

"Oh, no you wouldn't..."

Pushing and shoving, they went down the road that led to the village. Peppering the sky, a glittering paint-splash of stars blinked and winked, while away out over the sea the beam from the lighthouse returned the signal. There was a smell of ozone and rotting seaweed and it intermixed with the peaty tang of turf smoke to remind them that they were as far from city streets as the earth is from the sun.

"What d'you think of the country, Brooksie?" Hennessy asked his friend as they clumped along.

"It's okay, I suppose, but all this walking has my feet worn away to the knees. I wouldn't mind hailing a bus..."

"Think of all the exercise you're getting."

"I'm not into exercise."

"You'll lose weight."

"Ah, sure, amn't I grand as I am? John Candy is my hero, loose, jiggly and jolly...Remember what Big Julie said in that play we learned last year? 'Let me have men about me that are fat' he said. All them conspirators that stabbed him must've been thin as rakes..."

"Says who?"

"Stands to reason, doesn't it?"

They were beginning to encounter groups of students on their way to the céilí, most of them shying away when they caught sight of Hennessy. One lot even crossed over to the other side of the road, uttering little hoots of nervous laughter.

They came to the pub, An Súgán, and paused. Cars were parked every which way, and from the lighted windows, open to the night, drifted a pall of noise and cigarette smoke. Obviously the crowd was getting there on time.

"Getting the heebie-jeebies?" Brooks asked, a smirk on his face. "I'll bet you're sorry now you're not coming to the céilí with me..."

"Not at all," Hennessy said, braving it out. "I'm true to my friends, not like some people I could mention."

"If you think you're going to shame me into coming in with you, then you've another think coming. I'd stand out like a wart on a bald head..."

"Or a whale in a goldfish bowl?"

"Whatever." Brooks grinned in a superior way. "Sticks and stones may break my bones but insulting me'll get you nowhere. I've a hide as thick as a jockey's bottom..."

Hennessy sighed loudly. "Well, I guess this is the parting of the ways. If I don't return I hope you'll think of me kindly. And don't worry, I've left you my conker collection and my Hulk Hogan videos in my will..."

"Aw, for cryin' out loud..."

Brooks, obviously caught in two minds, stared at the sky, raised his fists on high, groaned audibly. "Decisions, decisions..." he said.

"You're going to come in with me, aren't you?" a delighted Hennessy crowed. "I knew you wouldn't let me down. You're like Roy Rogers' horse Trigger, only you're a two-footed friend..."

"Yeah," Brooks said resignedly, "and you know what happened to Trigger, don't you? He ended up being stuffed..."

The room that Swift and O'Brien had set up their equipment in was long and low, for all the world like a railway carriage. Entrance to it was gained by means of a stone passageway that led from the main pub. At the end of this passage a barrier had been erected and one of Joe Máire's minions, a skeleton-thin fellow with a nose long enough to poke a dog out from under a bed, sat behind it at a table and took the two pound admittance charge like a penguin gulping down fish.

Standing on the small stage at the end of the room, Swift beat out an experimental tattoo on one of his drums.

"The acoustics in here are awful," he told O'Brien.

"The wha?"

"Never mind."

Already the place was more than half full, the majority of the customers in various stages of intoxication. To Swift's critical eye they looked like a mob preparing to get up the courage to perform a lynching.

He stood up to the microphone and, to test it, coughed loudly. Immediately his magnified harump whammed off the ceiling and echoed round the railway carriage causing the audience to pause in whatever they happened to be doing and look sternly up at him.

"Sorry," Swift said, both to them and to a petrified O'Brien, then he fiddled with the sound box, causing it this time to emit a high-pitched whistle like a stone being drawn across slate.

A very drunk fellow in a tweed suit and matching cap made his way from the back of the hall and sat down with a thump at a table just under the noses of the musicians. He had a huge bandage on the index finger of his right hand and he kept this carefully pointing out in front of him like a direction finder. Looking up, he caught O'Brien's eye, and the wink that followed, executed in slow motion, contorted his face into a grinning effigy of evil.

"Might as well get on with it," Swift hissed. "Let's give them a blast of Anthrax's 'Anti-Social' and see how it grabs them."

They launched into it, the guitar whinnying and Swift's drumbeat adding a frenzied gallop. Halfway through, O'Brien forgot the words, but he continued mouthing into the mike, reeling off all he could think of at a moment's notice which were the lyrics of "Jingle Bells." He could have been reciting the Our Father for all the paying guests cared. After an initial stupefied silence, they began to shout and stamp their feet, with the sozzled character at the front waving his bandaged finger about as though conducting them.

The set ended to a chorus of catcalls and jeers, and a shower of beer mats came homing in on the unfortunate two on the bandstand. An enraged Joe Máire, his face a mask of malevolence, came stumping up from the back of the room, flailing his arms and shouting like a madman. Luckily for

Swift and O'Brien, the unhappy customers immediately turned their ire on the landlord, angrily cursing him and demanding their money back. It was beginning to look like the start of a riot when the tweed-suited drunk decided to take a hand, or, to be more precise, a finger, in affairs.

Jumping up on the table, he started roaring for "Ciúineas," overbalanced, fought the wobbling table manfully, then fell forward onto the floor, straight onto his injured digit.

His misfortune immediately appealed to the crowd's collective sense of humour and they began laughing instead of threatening murder and mayhem. Some wag shouted "Scaoil amach an bobailín," while another wanted to know if the band knew the song "Dropkick Me Jesus through the Goalposts of Life."

When an amount of quiet was restored, an old man at a corner table began playing the spoons, whacking them against his knee and knocking out a passable jig. Cocking his ear, O'Brien took up the run of the tune, then Swift joined in on the drums, and in no time the now jovial customers were clapping along in harmony. Urged on by a relieved Joe Máire, the duo on stage continued with "La Bamba"; then some more improvised jigs and reels, a jived-up version of "The Minstrel Boy," and a dose of country music songs that the audience sang along to with evident enjoyment.

By the end of the first half of the gig, Dave and Ned were well on their way to stardom and, when they finished with a flourish on "Molly Malone," they were applauded and whistled at, although not this time in derision but with approval.

By the time that Hennessy and Brooks managed to push their way into the hall, Swift and O'Brien were relaxing and taking the plaudits of their new fans. There was still an amount of uproar and the atmosphere was full of smoke and clatter. However, this suited the furtive two, as it was highly unlikely that either of them would be recognised in the prevailing conditions.

A bar had been opened up at one side of the room and the crush around it resembled a rugby scrum. The drunk with the finger had been resurrected and propped in a corner, and he leaned there like a warning to the other drinkers of the consequences of over-indulgence.

Hennessy and Brooks found it impossible to get near the musicians, who were being mobbed by a knot of eager would-be groupies.

"You see what I mean?" a red-faced Brooks cried. "It's a waste of time coming in here. Those two've eyes only for those girls..."

"Give them a chance. They haven't seen us yet. As soon as they do you'll see the light of gratitude for us being here in their eyes..."

Dave and Ned may not have spied Hennessy in his beret, raincoat and black face make-up but the drunk with the bandaged finger had. Obviously imagining that he had come across a kindred spirit, he pushed himself away from the wall, shouting, "Here, éistigí, éistigí..."

He caught up with Hennessy and stood swaying in front of him. "Arrah, muise, fair play dhuit a mhac," he warbled. "Let's have a little drink. Jest you and me..."

Draping an arm around the appalled Hennessy's neck, he began hustling him towards the mass of humanity around the bar, much to the amusement of a giggling Brooks.

"Get him off," Hennessy implored. "He's drawing attention to me. If any of the teachers are here we'll be up the creek without a paddle."

"He likes you," a chuffed Brooks responded. "You should be more friendly. Weren't we told to mix with the locals?"

"I think he's got designs on me," Hennessy wailed, grabbing at his beret, which had become dislodged under the drunk's attentions. Despairing of any other way of getting free, he suddenly sank his teeth into the bandaged finger which was hovering invitingly near his mouth.

The effect was immediate and electrifying. Uttering a loud screech like a banshee proclaiming the advent of a massacre, the unfortunate tippler dragged his violated hand free, then, holding it aloft like a trophy he had won, he went staggering off towards the exit. It was clear he felt that enough was enough and was off to a quieter spot to nurse his wounded digit and his pride in peace and solitude.

14

The two of them finally got through to Swift and O'Brien but, as Brooks had prophesied, the musicians were so flushed with their success that they had barely a word to spare for their two latest supporters.

Hennessy was outraged.

"After all the trouble I went to," he spluttered. "Disguising myself, wearing this stupid hat, this gooey soot, this...this..."

"Flasher's raincoat," Brooks supplied helpfully.

Hennessy glared at him.

"Well, it's your coat," he said, struggling to strip it off, "and you can bloody well carry it back."

"Not me," Brooks replied, backing off. "You wore it here; you look after it..."

A large man with a stomach protruding like a shelf bumped into Brooks from behind. He was carrying a trayful of drinks, some of which wobbled dangerously from the impact. He said something short and sharp in Irish, then translated it in case the meaning had been lost on the dismayed Brooks.

"Did you hear that?" Brooks asked his companion. "If my poor sainted mother could hear what her son's just been called she'd be lighting candles in the church until the whole place'd be lit up like Easter and Christmas rolled into one."

"Let's get outta here," Hennessy said. "It's dangerous even to stand in one place. Swiftie and Nedser are welcome to it..."

They left, passing the keeper of the gate who was arguing with a twosome who quite reasonably were demanding to be let in for half price considering that half the night was over. Ducking their way along the passage, they peered carefully into the main bar before crossing it, and finally emerged into the night that was as refreshing to their flushed countenances as a shower of rain is to a parched countryside.

"I don't know about you," Brooks said, "but I'm off to the céilí. Elsie'll be wondering where I am."

"Not to mention where the goodies are."

"Don't be like that."

"Did you ever wonder whether she liked you for your mind, your body or your chocolate collection?"

"Who cares?" Brooks shrugged. "At least she's got eyes only for me..."

Hennessy groaned.

"D'you have to bring that up again? I'd just about put it out of my mind..."

"Beware of Humphreys when they come bearing gifts. You can bet they're up to no good."

Hennessy spat on his hand and began rubbing at the soot on the lower part of his face. He succeeded only in moving it to areas where it hadn't been before.

"I can't go to the céilí done up like this," he

moaned. "I need to go back and take a shower. And by the time I do that the céilí'll be over anyway."

"Tough cheese."

Hennessy ducked as the headlights of a car sprayed over them but the vehicle passed on by and disappeared up the road. The night became as quiet again as a burglar's footfalls.

"You go on to the céilí," Hennessy said, "and I'll just moon around out here..."

"Moon?"

"In a manner of speaking. Dawdle, mooch, take a saunter. I know someone I can visit who'll be glad to see me."

"You mean your friend with the fickle finger of fate?"

"Don't be disgusting."

They parted: Brooks bound for the céilí, fingering the melting bars of chocolate in his pocket; Hennessy in the other direction, the raincoat now thrown over his shoulder, the beret at a rakish angle and the soot obliterating the lower half of his face, making it appear as if a pair of eyes was moving along unaided five feet four inches above the ground.

Out over the sea the moon, grinning as usual, had poked its way into the sky, and a hard-edged light was bathing the small stone pier and silvering the sides of the ancient tent where Jethro Cosgrave had taken up residence. The motorbike and the sidecar gave off little rattles and squeaks as the metal lost the heat of the day but otherwise all was a scene of peace and tranquillity.

The tide had come and gone but there was still enough water caught in the natural stone basin formed by the rocks to allow passage to the rubber dinghy that silently made its way in under the cover of the pier. The person in it was clothed completely in black, and was wearing a dark balaclava with eye, nose and mouth openings.

Making little more than a soft "tock," the rubber boat bumped against the stone steps leading up to the jetty. Quickly securing it to the iron spike provided, its occupant gathered up some pieces of equipment and carefully climbed upwards. Before letting himself be outlined against the sky, he took a bobbing glance over the edge, saw nothing to cause him anxiety and lightly vaulted on to the top of the pier.

Flattening himself out against the warm concrete, he paused for a minute or two to take stock of his surroundings. Nothing stirred, no alarm bells rang, no shouts of protest at this unwarranted intrusion were uttered.

Sure that he was unobserved, the dark figure half-scuttled, half-ran to the lee of the tent. A pair of bare feet stuck out under the badly tied flap and an indentation made by what was obviously a head could clearly be discerned in the canvas where a head should be in relation to the feet.

The intruder placed what he was carrying on

the ground, took a flexible rubber truncheon out of his belt and gave it a few experimental waggles. Softly he approached the bump in the patched canvas, measured his backswing and drew a forward blow with the cosh that ended with a solid thwack against flesh and bone. There was a groan from inside the tent, then silence.

Quickly the man went over to the motorbike, set up a plastic container and a length of rubber tubing and siphoned an amount of petrol out of the tank. This he sprinkled over the tent, the pungent odour of the fuel attacking the night air.

He then stuffed the opening of the petrol tank with a waxed gauze-like material, a length of which he led from the machine to the tent. Nonchalantly he tied this around the big toe of one of the protruding feet, and encircled the tent with the rest of it. When he was finished it looked as if a roll of toilet paper had come loose and draped itself where it had no business to be.

The petrol tank cap he hung on the top of the stick from which the tired Irish flag drooped.

Quickening his pace again, the mystery man went back to the dinghy and deposited the objects he had brought with him. Then he came back one more time. Surveying the scene, he seemed satisfied. There was the rasp of a match being lit, the end of the waxed material was ignited, the man stood to attention and mockingly saluted and the next moment he was away and running towards the edge of the jetty.

It took him only a couple of seconds to get into the rubber boat and a few more to clear the pier and row out into deeper water. Unable to resist one last look, he squinted back the way he had come and was just in time to see one of the seven dwarfs from *Snow White* come heigh-hoing over the crest of the rise and go marching down towards the ready-to-explode motorbike.

15

Hennessy was feeling sorry for himself, not something that happened very often. He felt hard done by: Swift and O'Brien were enjoying the fruits of their labours back in An Súgán, Brooks was eating and ogling back at the céilí and he was wandering around in the back of beyond, all done up like a dog's dinner and wearing a coat that was two sizes too big for him.

It didn't seem fair, somehow. After all, the only reason he had broken the rules was in order to go and applaud and give encouragement to the musical twosome in their hour of need. "Huh, some hour of need," he said aloud, then proceeded to trip yet again over the tail of Brooks' raincoat.

The coat was not his only problem; getting around by the coral strand and along the rocky coastline towards Jethro Cosgrave's tent by night, even if it was moonlit, was not as easy a prospect as doing it by day. The tide had left the rocks slippery and he had to be as nimble as a mountain goat to keep his footing at times. Then again, a pocket of shadow could just as well conceal a pool of scummy water as a solid place to put his foot.

He paused and took the coat off again and looped it once more over his shoulder. If he had given in to his feelings he would have thrown it into the sea. Near him the water sucked and lapped at the shore, while across the inlet he could see lights dotting the Clare coast.

Gazing ahead he figured that the pier beside which Jethro had pitched his tent was just over the crest of the next rise. He didn't really know why he had come. Was it to warn him? To ask him why he'd been loitering in the old graveyard? To tell him if he didn't start washing his socks more often his quota of visitors would be down to zero?

There was something about Jethro that appealed to the rebel in Hennessy. He was unusual, his own man, a space cadet. So many people looked the same, dressed the same, did the same things. All those bus and train loads of commuters going to work in the mornings and returning again at night. They were all so serious, like robots with little wheels and pulleys whirring away inside them. They very seldom smiled, laughed or stopped to put their eyes to a fence to see what was going on inside.

Hennessy himself never passed a hole in the ground without looking into it—sometimes he went the whole hog and fell into it! He was forever bumping into lampposts because his gaze was elsewhere; he eavesdropped on conversations, stuck his nose in where it wasn't wanted and generally made a nuisance of himself just because he was interested in everything that was going on about him.

And in Jethro Cosgrave he believed he recognised a fellow free-wheeling spirit, a man for all seasons, a head-the-baller—in short, a dirty eejit like himself.

Hoisting the coat to a more comfortable position, he continued on over the crest of the hill, at the same time jauntily singing:

"Heigh-ho, heigh-ho,
It's off to work we go,
With a shovel and a pick,
And a great big stick,
Heigh-ho, heigh-ho, heigh-ho."

If Hennessy was feeling sorry for himself, then Jethro Cosgrave was feeling even sorrier—for himself, that is. Dreaming of being president of Ireland, he had been stepping in seven-league boots over his tiny followers when a low-flying lump of black pudding, or some such unlikely object, had ambushed him and dealt him a violent blow on the back of his head.

Forced to take a rain-check on consciousness for a short period of time, he had awoken to a cascade of pain that danced in front of his eyes all got up in a ghastly shade of reddish purple. The Scarlet Pimpernel? And was he in heaven or was he in hell? Undoubtedly it was the fiery place, with little imps sticking pointed lances into his eyeballs and up his nose.

Gradually, above the pain, he heard someone groaning loudly: deep, from-the-heart expressions of genuine hurt. They were excruciating to listen to and he was about to protest when the thought came to him that possibly he himself was the one emitting these pitiful sounds. Surely not? he asked himself but when he held his breath to listen, the groaning ceased. Indubitably he was the responsible party.

Thinking that if he lay quietly, muttered a few aspirations and pretended he was someone else that the pain would go away, he composed himself and tried to empty his mind. And gradually, except for the woodpecker systematically knocking a hole in the back of his head, the rest of his tormentors slowly secreted their instruments of torture and crept away in search of fresh woods and pastures new.

From the top of the slope Hennessy could look down on the peaceful campsite and see everything that was to be seen. The motorbike was in place, so was the sidecar; the tent still looked a sorry sight, but at least it was standing; even the dilapidated rowing boat was morosely bobbing up and down as it had been the day before.

The only thing that was different was the small fire that was healthily blazing its way along the ground, indifferent to the fact that there was very little in the way of fuel for it to feed on.

"A moving campfire?" Hennessy wondered, knitting his brows. "Now that's a new one on me."

He decided to take a closer look and moved down the slope. Like a sportive animal, the fire danced gaily away from him. Then he noticed the strip of waxed cloth that the blaze was rapidly consuming. Staring, he saw the flame arc into the air, then hiss towards the big toe of a naked foot that was sticking out of the tent opening. It appeared that someone had arranged a hot foot for the sleeping Jethro.

The toe merely jiggled a bit, however, as the blaze encircled it, as though its owner was used to having his limbs singed. And obviously this was not the end of the practical joke, for the spark was now setting off again, this time in the direction of the motorbike and sidecar.

Curiously Hennessy followed along behind it, his whole attention so caught up that he did not notice the movement behind him until he was suddenly knocked over by a long lank form wearing only a pair of boxer shorts. This apparition started dancing on the naked flame, uttering wild war whoops as it did so and splitting the silence of the night apart.

From his reclining position, Hennessy felt like applauding the performance. It was fascinating to watch. No doubt Jethro, whom he now recognised, was engaged in some oriental folk-dance, perhaps in an attempt to ward off demons and hobgoblins. Or maybe he was putting in a bit of training in order to challenge an Indian holy man in a race over a bed of hot coals?

The fire finally out, Jethro ceased his hopping and came and sat down beside the giggling

Hennessy. Gingerly massaging the back of his head, he said, "'I am not at ease, nor am I quiet; I have no rest; but trouble comes,' Job, chapter 3: verse 26. You didn't by any chance bop me on the noggin, tie a live fuse round my toe and stick the other end into the petrol tank of my bike, did you? Because if you did I want you to know that I do not find it in the least bit funny."

"The petrol tank of your motorbike?" Hennessy asked, his giggles breaking off in mid-giggle.

"Take a look. I could've been blown to kingdom come."

Hennessy went over to the machine and inspected the petrol tank. The fuse was indeed stuffed into it. "You don't think I did that?" he said, eyeing Jethro warily across the short space of ground between them.

But Jethro had something else on his mind: "Why're you sporting a black beard all of a sudden?" he asked. "Have you aged prematurely since I saw you last?"

"It's not a beard, it's soot."

"Don't tell me, let me guess: you've hired yourself out as a boy chimney sweep?"

"It's a disguise."

"Well, it's not a very good one."

"I know that. But it's the only one I could think of at the time."

"And what time was that?"

"The time I was going to steal into the pub to see Swift and O'Brien make fools of themselves playing heavy rock for a bunch of Gaelgoiries..."

"Ah, I see it all now..."

Both of them lapsed into silence, sunk in their respective thoughts, then Hennessy said, "Why would someone want to kill you?"

Jethro looked at him. "I thought you might ask me that," he said. "Just give me a minute or two."

He went back to the tent, crawled in and, when he re-emerged, he was wearing a sweater and jeans and a pair of bright red socks. In his hand he was carrying a lit storm-lantern which he carefully secured in a crevice between two rocks. Immediately it was surrounded by a buzzing cloud of flying insects.

Hennessy was still gazing at the booby-trapped motorbike and Jethro came over and stood beside him.

"Why would someone want to do that?" Hennessy said again. He shivered suddenly.

Jethro scratched his head, then rubbed the stubble on his face. His hand made a rasping sound like sandpaper against rough plaster. "Hennessy, my friend," he said slowly, "I have to own up to the fact that I haven't been entirely open and frank with you. My name is indeed Jethro Cosgrave but I'm not a wandering man of the roads. In reality—whatever that might be—I'm Detective-Constable JT Cosgrave, serial number 6937, of the Anti-Drugs Squad, operating out of Store Street garda station and responsible to Superintendent Albert (Big Al) O'Donnelly and to the plain people of Ireland. In other words, I'm a copper."

"You're having me on."

"As God is my witness."

"And you're on an undercover operation," Hennessy breathed. "That's why you're dressed as a tramp..."

In the pale light from the storm-lantern, Jethro looked pained. "A tramp? This is the way I always dress. I thought I looked pretty snazzy."

"You do; you do," Hennessy hurriedly assured him. "But tell me more. What kind of deal is it you're investigating? Is it illegal poteen making?"

"Poteen making?"

"I saw you down at the old graveyard behind Miss Ó Fatharta's house last night. Brooks and I tried to follow you but you disappeared."

"I fell into a newly dug grave, if you must know."

Hennessy frowned. "We thought you'd gone down into the crypt. There's a whole warren of passages under it and one of them leads to the cave where Joe Máire, the owner of An Súgán, stores his booze."

"Really?" Jethro looked impressed. "You found out more than I did, so. I was covered in mud, so I went home."

"Some policeman you are," Hennessy scoffed.

"A case of 'The wise man has his eyes in his head but the fool walks in darkness.' Ecclesiastes, chapter 2: verse 14."

"What's with all this Bible-quoting? Are you making it up or what?"

"Well, it's like this. I met with an unfortunate accident once—to be honest, a villain shot me in a place that prevented me from sitting down. I ended up in traction in hospital for the best part of two months, and to pass the time I read the entire Bible. I happen to have a photographic memory, so..."

"Pretty ropey, if you ask me."

"You don't believe me?"

"It doesn't matter," Hennessy said dismissively. "But you were going to tell me what brought you to Tóin le Gaoith...?"

"Was I?"

"Come on, you owe it to me."

Jethro made the filing sound again with his stubble. "I suppose I do," he admitted. "If I hadn't gone out to see who was there when you came along, I'd probably be barbecued spare ribs by now."

"Okay then, give..."

"Well, as I told you, I'm with the anti-drugs squad, so obviously it's a drugs bust I'm after. It's got nothing to do with poteen making, legal or otherwise."

"I didn't think there was any such thing as legal poteen making."

"You should try to convince the people around here that."

"So, what kind of drugs?"

"Cocaine. How the wealthy and well-to-do get their kicks nowadays. Nose candy. A bit of crack..."

"I have heard of it."

"Yes, well..." Jethro looked up as the lamp waned but it was only a stray breeze insinuating itself behind the glass panel. He went on, "I've been on the trail of a certain gentleman now for quite a while, a go-boy who supplies half the dealers on the east coast. Upwardly mobile he is, keeps a smart front, good clothes, expensive car..."

"High-powered speedboat?"

"That's right. The stuff is brought across the Atlantic by steamer. He goes out to meet it and brings the product in by night...How'd you know about the speedboat?"

Hennessy spread his hands. "Elementary, my dear Watson. I know exactly who you're talking about. I wondered how he could afford such expensive toys on a teacher's salary. It's Seán de Burca, isn't it?"

"That's correct. A slippery character. I've been after him for the best part of two years. He's not the only supplier but he's one of the biggest and the cutest. And he aims to keep up his lucrative business..."

"You mean he was the one who tried to kill you?"

"I can't think of a likelier candidate, unless it was the Holy Ghost trying to guard the copyright of the Bible."

Hennessy absentmindedly rubbed his nose,

leaving a generous smear of soot behind. "Maybe I can help you nab him," he said. "I could watch him for you."

Jethro shook his head.

"No, I don't want you to get involved. de Burca may appear to be a charmer but there's a deadly side to him. A couple of his competitors met with nasty accidents last year that led to a terminal shortness of breath. de Burca had an alibi each time but he's still the prime suspect."

"I'm finding this hard to believe," Hennessy said, after a short pause. "de Burca is my teacher. He's been nice to me, took me out in his boat, listened to my problems. You, on the other hand, are a highly suspicious-looking lad, tall, unshaven, that long coat..."

"You can't blame me for being tall. Just because you're a squirt."

"...and you've acted in a highly questionable manner ever since you've been here. How do I know that you're not the drug smuggler and that de Burca isn't the policeman?"

"Because I'm the one that was bopped on the head and offered as a sacrifice to the god of microwaves..."

"You could've set that up yourself to divert suspicion. You put the fuse out fairly handily."

"Only because you came along."

"I wonder."

"Aw, come off it." Jethro walked away in his red socks. Then he turned and came back again. "If I did plan this business of the attempt on my life, who was I trying to impress? You? I didn't even know you'd be along here tonight. There's an ass in the adjoining field. You think it was for his benefit? I ask you..."

"Okay, okay," Hennessy conceded, "I admit someone did try to maim you or worse. All the more reason why you could do with a bit of help."

Jethro stopped to consider, then he said, "Right, you can keep an eye on de Burca for me but don't make it too obvious. And do it only during the day. I'll take over at night."

"D'you carry a gun?"

"No, I don't carry a gun. Who d'you think I am? Clint Eastwood?"

"I know someone who does."

"Does what?"

"Think you're Clint Eastwood. My friend Brooks mistook you for him last night."

"Is that so?"

Moodily Jethro kicked at the ground, then winced when it was borne home to him that he wasn't wearing any shoes. Limping back towards the tent, he said over his shoulder, "I'm going to lie down now and rest my weary head. And remember: 'He who keeps his mouth and his tongue, keeps himself out of trouble.' That's from Proverbs, chapter 21: verse 23."

"And a jolly goodnight to you too," said Hennessy, as the flap fell behind the departing figure of Constable JT Cosgrave, Bible-thumper and minion of the law.

16

The rest of the week went by uneventfully. There was a full round of classes and other activities each day to keep everyone busy, and Hennessy threw himself wholeheartedly into improving his Irish.

His relationship with Kitty blew hot and cold: some days she was all over him while on other days he hardly merited a glance. Brooks was managing to hold Elsie's interest, although the contents of his formerly bulging suitcase were rapidly dipping towards the minus area.

They saw very little of Swift and O'Brien but heard a great deal about them. They had attained the status of minor celebrities and An Súgán had the "house full" signs posted most nights. It was said that Joe Máire had been seen to smile twice in one day and it was rumoured that someone else had spied him patting the crossroads' dog rather than kicking it.

All of the following day after his talk with Jethro Hennessy had kept his secret but by evening the temptation to tell someone had finally gnawed away at his resolve and he took Brooks into his confidence.

"You have to swear you won't tell anyone," he told him. "Cross your heart and hope to die and all that. Jethro put me under the great oath of the seven snotty orphans."

"You expect me to believe what that goonie told you?" Brooks said, looking singularly unimpressed. "I wouldn't be surprised if he's in the DTs from drinking contraband poteen..."

"But I was there. I saw the set-up. If I hadn't come along he'd've been blown to smithereens."

"So what're you going to do? Are you going to skulk around spying on de Burca like a reincarnation of Maxwell Smart? You'll look a right clown if your man Jethro is having you on."

In fact, Hennessy soon grew tired of his "Watchman, what of the night?" routine, for de Burca behaved in a completely normal fashion and did nothing whatever out of the ordinary. He taught his classes, took the pupils on excursions in the afternoons, supervised them at night at the various functions. He laughed, joined in with whatever fun was going, and proved by far to be the most popular of the teachers.

There were a few minor hiccups on the course: one fellow, a particularly scatter-brained lout, got caught in a current one day and had to be rescued from drowning by Tommy Ugly himself; a girl had her purse stolen and a fellow-student was suspected but it turned out later that she had merely mislaid it; and to Hennessy's great joy his rival, Humphrey, was caught smoking and was confined to barracks for three full nights.

The weather held good: long sunny days, calm

seas and clean, blue-rinsed views of, in one direction, the Aran Islands, and, in the other, the jagged-toothed peaks of the Twelve Pins. City pallor was replaced by healthy browns and old-gold yellows, although a few of the more fair-skinned suffered in their pursuit of tans, and one red-haired girl had to be whisked away in an ambulance to hospital such was the severity of her sunburn.

On the Friday evening, however, wicked-looking clouds began to barrel in over the sea and soon there were dancing flickers of lightning decorating the horizon. It became very hot and stuffy, and thunder rumbled ominously.

It came as a relief when the rain suddenly belted down in a deluge as if some great dam in the sky had given way. All that night it poured, and the Saturday morning dawned grey and misty, the landscape saturated, the gutters running with water.

As Hennessy and Brooks made their way towards the school they had to jump like grasshoppers to avoid the slashes of water thrown up by passing cars. They were still only halfway there when one of these vehicles pulled up beside them.

It was Seán de Burca, and he gestured to them to climb in. It didn't seem to bother him that their wet clothes and muddy feet would play havoc with the shining interior of the Saab.

"Tá sé fliuch," he greeted them, "ach tá aimsear bhreá ar an mbealach..."

Although his Irish was improving, Hennessy

was still a bit unsure in the medium, so he sat back and let Brooks carry on the conversation. As the two of them talked, he took the opportunity to observe de Burca more closely.

For a man who, according to Constable Jethro, was a dyed-in-the-wool crook, a villain who supplied one of the deadliest drugs to the people he had ensnared, he appeared quite carefree and devoid of any pangs of conscience. Attired in a leather jacket and matching cap he looked the very picture of what he was supposed to be: a responsible member of society contentedly on his way to work. Compared to him, Jethro looked a right old reprobate, a misfit, a guy you wouldn't exactly trust to carry your money to the bank for you.

de Burca and Brooks were discussing the fancy dress masquerade that was to be held in the hall that night. It was a traditional Saturday-evening event and it had been mentioned in the brochure so that people could bring their costumes with them if they so wished.

Hennessy's grandmother, Molly Caskey, had wanted him to wear the court jester's uniform he had worn in the school musical but he had managed to persuade her that it should be kept in mothballs and preserved for posterity for his children's children. He had had enough of that particular costume to last him a lifetime.

A number of students were clustered outside the school building, making the most of the last few minutes of freedom before the bell rang to call them to class. When they alighted, Kitty and Elsie broke away from a clatter of girls and came over to them.

They were full of the fancy dress.

"What're you going to wear?" Kitty asked, her eyes shining under the quickened impetus of the possibility of dressing up.

"I'm going as Genghis Khan," Brooks said. "And I've got one of those trick nails—you know the ones that seem to be going right through your head...?"

"I thought Genghis Khan was the one that hammered in the nails, rather than the opposite?"

"Ah, but he came to a sticky end himself," Brooks said airily. "It was Attila the Hun done him in..."

"Haven't you a few centuries mixed up there?" Hennessy asked him. "Attila was long gone before Genghis came on the scene. They called him 'The Scourge of God.'"

"Who?"

"Attila the Hun."

"I don't think I wish to know that."

Elsie giggled, then held her hand in front of her face as if the giggle had taken her by surprise.

"What about you, Henno?" Kitty asked him. "What'll you reveal to us on the night?"

"He's going in the Emperor's New Clothes," Brooks said. "That way he'll be able to reveal all."

There was a chorus of sniggers which Hennessy disdainfully ignored. "I shall come as a pirate," he said, standing on his dignity. "A buccaneer of the Spanish Main. Maybe as Sir Henry Morgan..."

"Was he Redbeard?" Kitty asked. "If so you could cut some of your hair off and glue it to your chin."

"My hair stays firmly on my head," Hennessy said, this time to a barrage of hoots.

The girls informed them that they were dressing up as punks: they were going to put gel in their hair, safety-pins in their ears, and wear enough chains to make a ghost turn red with envy.

Further conversation was stifled by the jangle of the school bell and they shuffled along into the various classrooms. The last of them had just gone inside when a sudden gust of wind blew down the deserted road, and in its wake, with coat-tails flapping and riding a bicycle several sizes too small for him, came the singular figure of Jethro Cosgrave. He appeared to be in a hurry...

Hennessy was finding the morning lesson heavy going. It dealt with the intricacies of the genitive case in Irish, a state of affairs with which he had only a passing acquaintance. Idly he looked around, caught Kitty's eye and stuck his tongue in the corner of his mouth and rolled his eyes back into his head. She frowned and glanced quickly away.

He was sitting beside the window, so he peered out to see if there was anything abroad that might interest him. All that met his gaze was a sight of the opposite wall of the school building and Tommy

Ugly's figure framed in a window as he taught a class.

He was about to turn back to affairs in his own room when his view was obscured by what appeared to be a disembodied head rising slowly from below the sill of his own window. A face that only a mother could love looked in at him and a bloodshot eye winked in a most evil and lewd manner.

He gazed at it in horror, then noticed that it was signalling to him with its eyebrows. It didn't take him long to come to the conclusion that it wished to have an audience with him outside. When he nodded, it slowly sank from view, the Excalibur of Tóin le Gaoith.

After a pause, he raised his hand, caught de Burca's attention and asked, "An bhfuil cead agam dul amach?"

Permission being granted, he rose and made his way past Brooks' inquiring look towards the door. No one else paid him the slightest attention.

In case anyone was watching, he paid a quick visit to the toilet, then hastily slid out a side door. The yard was deserted except for a seagull which was forlornly looking for scraps.

Tiptoeing round a corner, he beheld the long figure of Jethro Cosgrave clinging by his fingertips to the sill of the window of the classroom. He was standing on the saddle of what looked like a child's bicycle and his balance was precarious, to say the least.

Hennessy moved up closer, then whispered "Hi."

Too late he realised that he should have made his presence known in a more circumspect manner for, as soon as he heard Hennessy's "Hi" behind him, Jethro jerked like a puppet whose string had been pulled. This movement activated the bicycle, which shot out from under him, went scooting along by the wall and disappeared round the corner.

For one glorious moment Jethro was suspended in the air, like a character in a cartoon, a look of comical dismay on his face. Then, in a flurry of arms and legs, he rapidly descended, to land with a sodden thump in what had been a moment before a well-ordered flower-bed. There he sprawled, an intruder in the muck.

He looked at Hennessy, Hennessy gazed back at him. In some situations words are unnecessary and indeed superfluous but Jethro was never the man to remain silent even on the stickiest of occasions.

Easing himself into a more comfortable position, he said resignedly, "Jesus wept..."

17

"What's so urgent then that you have to call me out of class?" Hennessy asked Jethro, as they crouched down beside the demolished flower-bed. The rain had finally stopped but everywhere was still saturated and Hennessy could feel the dampness seeping into the seat of his trousers from the wet grass.

"de Burca is going out tonight," his companion whispered conspiratorially. "I've had a tip-off from Dublin. My boss, Big Al himself, is on his way down but he'll keep out of sight until the right moment."

"What about the local guardians of the law? Are they not going to be involved?"

"They've been briefed, but they've also been told to act only as back-up. Big Al wants the glory of this bust all for himself."

"So why're you telling me?"

"I don't want you getting caught up in it, that's why. As of now, you're off the case. From this on you can safely leave it to the professionals."

"What professionals?" Hennessy asked, drawing back and doing a critical survey of the mud plastered to Cosgrave's long length.

Jethro looked hurt. "Accidents can happen," he

said. "Nobody's perfect."

"Where'd you get the bicycle?"

This time he looked evasive.

"I...ah...I borrowed it."

"Some poor kid's probably going around bawling looking for it. The bad guy drives about in a super-charged Saab and you ride around on a toy bicycle. Who says crime doesn't pay?"

"Well, you pays your money...Anyway, I want you to swear to me that you won't interfere in tonight's happenings. This is the wind-up of nearly two years' work and if I blow it I'll be back walking the beat."

"Couldn't I just watch from a distance?"

"Yes, if from a distance means from your bedroom window."

"But de Burca moors his boat at the jetty at Trá Bhán and that's about a mile from where I'm staying."

"Exactly."

Now it was Hennessy's turn to look hurt. "After all the help I've given you," he said bitterly, "and now when the showdown comes I'm left minding the horses. Don't you think I deserve a bit more than that?"

"I'll mention you in dispatches. I'll get you a leather medal. I'll put you up for an award for gallantry in action. But just stay away tonight. Isn't there a fancy dress parade? Go to that. Enjoy yourself. And tomorrow morning I'll seek you out and tell you all about it. That's fair, isn't it?

Remember 'It is better for a man to hear the rebuke of the wise than to hear the song of fools.' Ecclesiastes, chapter 7: verse 5."

"What's that supposed to mean?"

"I'm not sure, but it sounded right. Promise?"

Hennessy scowled, then between gritted teeth he said, "Okay, I promise."

"Good man."

Jethro stood up. Rivers of muddy water ran down off his waxed coat and his boots resembled the ones Charlie Chaplin tried to eat in the film *The Gold Rush*. He was a sorry sight.

Stooping, he made his way to the corner around which the bicycle had disappeared. Before he moved from view he glanced back and the look he saw on Hennessy's face made him more than a little uneasy. It could only be described as pensive...

"I wish I had some fake blood," Brooks said, inspecting himself in the mirror.

They were in the bedroom of their digs getting ready for the fancy dress ball. The trick nail appeared to be embedded in his forehead, with the point protruding from the back of his head.

"I could provide you with some real blood, if you like," Hennessy offered.

"Oh?"

"Your own, I mean, not mine. Just a little nick in that big vein at the base of your thumb and you'd have a geyser of it."

"Thanks very much, but no way..."

Hennessy was wearing a scarf that Kitty had lent him tied bandana-fashion round his head and one of Brooks' Hawaiian shirts. He had his jeans tucked into a pair of bright orange knee-socks. Through his belt was poked a rather sorry-looking sword that he had cut out of a piece of stiff cardboard.

"I feel like a right fool," he said. "These things always seem like a great idea until the actual time comes to dress up. Then you realise what a clodhopper you're making of yourself."

"Aw, when you see the rest of them you won't feel so bad," Brooks consoled him. "You'll fade into the scenery..."

As well as the nail he himself was attired in a white surplice, a leftover from his days as an altar boy, and a pair of Aladdin slippers with curled-up toes that his mother had thoughtfully packed for him. If the occasion arose where he had to run fast, he'd be done for.

Hennessy had told Brooks about his conversation with Jethro Cosgrave, but he was still sceptical. Now he came back to the subject again.

"I hope you don't intend doing anything stupid tonight," he said. "It could be a dangerous business."

"About Humphrey you mean?"

"No, I don't mean about Humphrey. The Cosgrave and de Burca affair."

"That thought never crossed my mind."

"Hah!"

"You don't believe me?"

"I know you too well. You just have to stick your nose in. Some day it'll get cut off."

"Are you worried about me?"

"No, just about your nose."

Hennessy caught hold of the said object, looking thoughtful. "Well, if I do happen to wander down around Trá Bhán I'll be fully armed," he said.

With that he made to pull the fake sword out of his belt and the handle came away in his hand.

Brooks gave an ass's bray of a laugh: "That'll surely put the fear of God into de Burca," he said. "He'll be so frightened he'll hand over the drugs, the boat and his lucky St Christopher medal..."

Looking sheepish, Hennessy said, "Stranger things have happened. Arnold Schwarzenegger is supposed to be afraid of mice..."

The students on the course had really put their all into dressing-up and the school hall was a swirl of oddly costumed and exotic creations. Vampires leered at milkmaids; creatures in long dresses and eyes ringed by black mascara talked to boys in shorts carrying tennis rackets; Superman and Batman were present; so were a couple of ninja turtles, a brace of Hulk Hogans and a scattering of Michael Jacksons.

Music was provided by a portable disco, and the DJ presiding over it had got into the spirit of the occasion by wearing a black body-stocking outlined skeleton-fashion in white paint. The thunder of the Rolling Stones' "Rock and a Hard Place" appeared to be making his bones rattle.

Hennessy and Brooks pushed their way through the crowd, looking for a pair of punk rockers. The problem was that most punks look the same and, after hailing the same two for the third time as Kitty and Elsie and finding that they were mistaken, they were beginning to despair of ever finding the right couple.

"We'll split up," Hennessy shouted above the din. "Meet back at the door if either of us has any success."

He dived back into the rabble and had only gone a short distance when he spied a couple dancing, the girl a punk, the fellow wearing only his trousers, his upper body covered in green paint. Obviously he was meant to be the Incredible Hulk. He did have a pretty good build, Hennessy admitted to himself. He saw to his dismay that it was Humphrey, his rival in the girl stakes. It didn't need much further brain work on his part to put two and two together and come up with Kitty as the punk dancing partner.

Hennessy went across and did his best to insinuate himself between them. He did receive some crumb of comfort when he perceived that Humphrey's body paint had not properly dried and that large blobs of it were becoming attached to anyone who happened to brush up against him.

"How's it going," Hennessy shouted, trying at the same time to poke his cardboard sword between Humphrey's legs and trip him up.

Kitty raised her eyes at him and grinned. Her
hair had been coaxed into rigid spikes, a razor-
blade dangled from one ear, a safety-pin from the
other, and she was jangling enough chains to keep
an escape artist busy for a whole weekend.

"Can't complain," she mouthed at him, taking
evasive action as another splatter of evil-looking
green paint detached itself from Humphrey's torso
and went looking for a suitable target. Brooks
looming up on the starboard bow got it right in
the middle of his white surplice.

Soon Humphrey was dancing by himself in a
cleared space as the rest of the company fell back
to get away from the shower of green rain. Hennessy
took the opportunity to steer Kitty towards the
refreshments area at the side of the hall and they
were joined there by Brooks and Elsie.

"What d'you think of the outfit?" Hennessy
asked, lowering his voice when he realised he was
still shouting.

Kitty looked him up and down.

"What're you supposed to be?"

"A pirate, of course. What'd you think?"

"You should've worn a patch over your eye. Or
borrowed a wooden leg."

"A parrot, now," Brooks put in slyly, "that'd
really set off the costume."

"No, no parrots," Hennessy cried, recoiling in
horror—he was remembering his grandmother's
pet parrot, Mabel, and the chaos it had created at
the final rehearsal of the school play: not alone

had it attacked the music teacher but it'd then perched on a roof rafter and crapped on anyone who tried to coax it down.

The night wore on, and it was around ten o'clock when Hennessy, who had been keeping a weather eye on Seán de Burca, saw him quietly leave the hall by one of the side doors. Kitty and Elsie had sloped off to the Ladies and Brooks was once more out guzzling lemonade and crisps in the makeshift shop.

Doing his best to appear inconspicuous, Hennessy made his way along by the wall to the same door that de Burca had left by. Just as he was about to slip out he met Humphrey. He had washed the green paint off but he still radiated a slight tinge. He looked so miserable that Hennessy almost felt sorry for him.

18

The rain clouds had gone and the night was clear and starry. Hennessy thought about mounting his bicycle like the cowboys in the old movies with a flying leap into the saddle but regretfully decided not to on the grounds that he could do himself irreparable damage. Instead he got aboard in the time-honoured fashion and went speeding down the road like a shot off a shovel.

The road to Trá Bhán led down by the Gaelic pitch, along by the comprehensive school and in between a pair of massive stone pillars that probably had once supported iron gates. There was a strip of hard-packed soil to allow cars to turn, a rock-strewn stretch of beach and a small cement jetty. This jetty was usually cluttered with nets set out to dry, lobster pots and empty, foul-smelling fish baskets.

Hennessy had visited it a couple of times just by way of variety but the seaweed-choked water was not pleasant to swim in and he had gone back the second time only to show Brooks de Burca's sleek and powerful boat.

Now he dismounted beside the pillars, shoved the bicycle in beside one of them and left the road and took to the fields. Clumps of bracken proved difficult to get through and head-high brambles did their best to pluck out his eyes. As he got closer to the beach he tried to go more carefully, crouching down and feeling his way with extreme caution.

The foliage became more scattered and, so that he would not be outlined against the sky, he crawled the last few yards. He had come out slightly to the right of the pier but from his elevated position he had a good view along its length.

de Burca's boat was moored at the furthest point, a dark bulk against the starshine on the water. There was no sign of movement, none of the little rattles and bangs which signify that a boat is being got ready for sea. The only thing to disturb the silence of the night was the gentle suck and sway of the water against the pilings of the jetty.

Hennessy wondered where Jethro was. Surely he should be around somewhere, keeping an eye on things? Could he have been disguised as one of the stone pillars? No, he thought, actually shaking his head although no one could see him, that's a bit too out of sight even for him.

Come to that, there was no sign of de Burca either. Scratching his head, Hennessy wondered what he should do. As he saw it, he had three choices. He could stay where he was and wait for something to happen, he could return to the hall, or he could go down and have a scout around the boat. The first would be the reasonable thing to do, the second would be the right thing to do, and the third would probably get him scalped.

Naturally he decided on the third...

Down on the jetty the ozone smell of the sea was tainted by the scent of rotting fish and drying seaweed. The shrouded shapes of the nets were like old women squatting in sleep and draped in their shawls. Using these and whatever else happened to afford shelter, Hennessy did a zig-zag along the pier, the brittle scrunch of sea-salt harsh beneath his feet. The concrete was still slippery from the recent rain. and he had to be careful not to get too close to the edge in case he did a nosedive into the black and choppy water.

He came to the bow of the boat. It was riding high, a sign that the tide was in. Gently it thudded against the dock and, when he looked down, he could just make out the tyre suspended from its side that kept it from being damaged by the concrete wall.

A dim light was showing in the wheelhouse but otherwise the vessel was in darkness. He waited, holding his breath, but no one came to challenge him, to ask him what his business was or to send him away with a flea in his ear.

Time passed. Once, as he gazed at the sky, a star fell, a long snail-track of light that gradually faded. When he was smaller his Grandmother Caskey had tried to convince him that it was a soul on its way to heaven, but now, to his dubious way of thinking, it was going in the opposite direction.

Eventually deciding that he would have to make a move before he became paralysed, he vaulted lightly over the side of the boat. The deck rocked gently under his sneakered feet but otherwise he caused as much commotion as a snowflake slowly falling and falling slowly. The little twang he heard he put down to his nerve ends jangling together.

He crept along the deck, skirted the hatch and sneaked a glance into the deckhouse. It was as deserted as a bald head. The wheel was anchored into place by a bright steel lock and the instrument panel was dark and featureless.

"Seems there's no one aboard," he said out loud, just to hear the murmur of his own voice. It sounded thin and reedy and slightly cracked.

Back he went to the hatch, hesitated a moment, then put his foot on the first rung of the ladder. Remembering the film *Aliens* he half expected a slimy tentacle to wrap itself round his ankle. Nothing of the kind occurred, so he slowly descended. When he got to the bottom he waited until his eyes became accustomed to the dark. Eventually he was able to make out that he was standing in what was probably the main cabin. It was much roomier than he would have thought, with two bunk beds, one on top of the other, a formica-topped work bench cum counter cum table, and a couple of easy chairs with fold-down backs bolted to the floor.

An arched entrance led to another, smaller cabin and he stuck his head in to have a look. It was stacked with boxes, fishing gear and various odds and ends. A wet suit was hanging from a wire hanger, like a skin that had been shed by some denizen of the deep.

Hennessy poked around, puzzled by the fact that the boat was so deserted. The awful thought came to his mind that Jethro might have been leading him up the garden path—telling him that the point of departure was here, while the real business was being conducted elsewhere. To get me out of the way, he thought resentfully. The long tall Sally!

He was about to give up in disgust and go back to the dance when he heard a sound that anchored him where he was as surely as if his feet had become nailed to the floor. It was a long, hollow moan, almost comical in its resemblance to the kind used in films to scare funny men like Laurel and Hardy or Abbot and Costello. Now, however, in the context of the dark and seemingly deserted boat, it raised the hairs on the back of Hennessy's head as if they had suddenly come alive.

When power was restored to his brainbox, his first reaction was to take off as fast as his feet would carry him. But then his innate stubbornness got the better of him and he peered suspiciously around with the thought that someone was trying to have him on. It would be just like Jethro, or de Burca for that matter, to play such a trick on him and then sit back and laugh about it.

"No way, Jose," he said aloud. "I'm not budging,

so you'd better come out wherever you are..."

By way of answer another moan reverberated round the cabin, this one sounding a little more authentic than the first. To Hennessy's fevered imagining, it appeared to seep out of the very wall.

He started searching, looking in and under both bunks, examining the space behind the counter, even pulling the plug in the stainless steel sink and peering down to see if he could spy an eye looking back at him. He could find nothing.

Exhausting the possibilities of the main cabin, he went back inside the smaller one and turned it over. Again he came up with zilch. Whoever or whatever was haunting the boat had found a good hiding place—certainly one that he couldn't uncover.

He returned to the main cabin and gave it another going over. This time he found an odd-looking strap hanging from the wall opposite the bunk beds. It didn't appear to be a switch for a light: it was merely a piece of leather with an eyelet that was fixed to a button embedded in the wall.

He toyed with it, flicking it this way and that, trying to work up the courage to pull it. It could be anything, maybe even a siren to give warning that there was an interloper on board.

He gave it a gentle tug. Nothing. He pulled a little harder. Still nothing. Ah, to hell with it, he thought, and he bore down on it with all his might.

Immediately the whole wall appeared to come away from the bulkhead, stood poised for a moment, then whacked onto the floor of the cabin with a resounding crash. Hennessy had hit the jackpot with his third pull.

19

From his vantage point on the top bunk, up on to which he had jumped in fright at the collapsing wall, Hennessy looked down on what he now perceived was a fold-up bed. And the reason it had come so thunderously out of its alcove was that it was occupied.

Jethro Cosgrave was tied to it, arms and legs outstretched, head lolling forward. He appeared to be well and truly out for the count.

The crash had not brought anyone running, so Hennessy cautiously climbed down from his perch and approached the bound and gagged figure. Sniffing, he recognised from his chemistry set days the odour of chloroform: the manly policeman had clearly been zonked with it and was likely to remain unconscious for the foreseeable future.

Once again Hennessy scratched his head. Jethro must have been surprised and rendered insensible by de Burca, who was now possibly lurking somewhere near at hand awaiting further incursions onto his territory. Then again, if he was on guard duty, how had he missed Hennessy's less than noiseless entry? Probably after assaulting Jethro he had gone back to the fancy dress to let himself be seen and thus establish an alibi. In that case, he would be back soon, to make sure his prisoner was still sleeping the sleep of the just and to complete the business of picking up the cocaine from his source at sea.

As though Hennessy had plugged into de Burca's thought processes, he immediately heard footsteps on the deck above his head. They were quiet and careful but unmistakable. And they were not the footfalls of a jolly sailor coming back from a night on the town.

Quickly Hennessy looked around, trying to decide what to do. He would never be able to get the bed back into place, so he would have to depend on de Burca believing that it was Cosgrave's weight that had caused it to fall out of the wall. As for himself, he would have to find somewhere to hide and as soon as possible if not sooner. The space under the bunk was not deep enough for him to be obscured from the view of someone descending the ladder. There were no cupboards or containers big enough to hold him: everything was too compact and too stowed away.

With a glance over his shoulder, he scurried into the inner cabin. The wet suit beckoned to him. Unzipping it, he hurriedly climbed into its rubbery embrace, first having to discard the cardboard sword that was still poking through his belt. The suit was several sizes too big for him, but this was a blessing as its loose folds made it still seem to be uninhabited. He crouched down, pulled the zipper back up and hoped for the best.

An interminable amount of time went by before he heard the squeak of rubber-soled shoes on the hatchway ladder. Deciding to chance it, he lowered the fastening again slightly and looked out. In the dim light he could see the glimmer of de Burca's fashionable curls and the flash of his expensively capped teeth.

He stood looking about him; then he approached the bed and began testing Jethro's bindings. Satisfied, he straightened up again, threw another cursory glance round the cabin and went back up the ladder. For the moment at least, Hennessy was safe.

Whether it was the relaxing of tension or what, as soon as he had disappeared from sight Hennessy's twitching nostrils exploded, and he sneezed, once, twice, three times. To his dismay, they sounded like bomb blasts in the confines of the cabin.

More time passed but he stayed where he was and thought that he now knew what it was like to be buried alive. Then, with a suddenness that made him sneeze again, the engine thudded into life, coughed a few times and settled into a healthy rumble. Soon after that he felt a tremble in the floor and surmised that the boat was moving away from the jetty.

Believing that de Burca would be unlikely to come below again while the vessel was in motion, he struggled out of the clammy clasp of the suit. As he did so the boat surged forward and he went stumbling backwards until his progress was halted by something that poked sharply into his back. He turned, to discover a harpoon gun hanging from a ratchet, small and compact but deadly when loaded.

He pulled it from its mounting and hefted it. It was lighter than he expected. Investigating further he found a plastic container and when he screwed off the top two of the foot-long bolts that the gun fired fell out at his feet. He picked one up and examined it. One end was wickedly pointed and had the shape of an arrowhead, while the other was flanged and held an aperture to contain the cord that trailed out behind it and enabled it to be drawn back along with whatever small or large fish it happened to transfix.

He loaded the harpoon into the gun. Then, holding it in front of him, he ventured out into the main cabin. Jethro was still supine on the bed, his head now thrown back, his eyes half closed so that the whites could barely be seen. It was clear that he was still far from regaining full consciousness. He was about as useful to Hennessy as his cardboard sword.

He sat down on the edge of the lower bunk, the gun in his lap. There was very little he could do except hope that de Burca, after collecting the drugs, would return to Trá Bhán. But then again, he was no fool and he would realise that Jethro wasn't working alone. It was much more likely that he would head for some other secluded spot along the coast, ditch the boat and take off with his ill-forgotten gains.

Supposing he decided to scuttle the boat, don the wet suit and swim ashore? That would leave Jethro and himself in a pretty pickle: they'd be playing tag in Davy Jones' locker.

Hennessy got up and went over to the porthole and looked out. The boat was well out from land and all he could see was an occasional whitecap as the powerful craft surged through the water. He decided to bide his time. After all, there was the possibility that a police boat might be circling in the vicinity waiting to pounce on de Burca and whoever was bringing in the cocaine. If that was the case, then all his worrying would have been in vain.

He glanced at his watch and saw that it was nearly midnight. He had barely registered the fact when the engine of the boat abruptly ceased and, in the silence, he heard voices call out in some foreign language. Back he went to the porthole but the other craft must have been on the opposite side to where he was looking out and again he could see nothing but rolling sea.

Cursed with curiosity, he went quietly up the ladder and took a quick dekko over the rim of the hatch. de Burca's boat was bobbing up and down in the lee of a large, modern-looking vessel, one with a radar tower and a number of high-tech antennae jutting out of it. As he watched, the boom from a winch came swinging down, a plastic-covered parcel attached to it. After a number of attempts, de Burca managed to grab hold of it and shake the package free. He crouched over it and there was the flash of a knife as he cut through the fastenings.

Evidently satisfied by what he found, he tied what looked like an attaché case to the boom; the winch whined and both boom and its burden went slicing back towards the other boat. A few more pleasantries were exchanged; then de Burca went back inside the wheelhouse, the engine roared and they veered away from the other craft and headed, Hennessy hoped, back the way they had come.

He returned and took up his former position on the bunk. Another twenty minutes dragged by, then once more the engine was cut and the boat started to drift. When he heard footsteps approaching the hatch he went into the other cabin and stood just inside the archway with the harpoon gun held aloft. de Burca might not be as big as a whale but at this range he would still provide a reasonably ample target.

Now he was moving about in the main cabin and, by the sound of his exertions, he was giving Jethro a helping hand to stand up. There was an amount of scuffling and heavy breathing and, when Hennessy chanced a peek around the corner, he was just in time to see Cosgrave's feet disappearing up through the hatch.

On tippy-toes Hennessy followed, crouched below the opening and took a deep breath, and then ducked his head out to have a look at what was going on. de Burca had Jethro draped over the side of the boat so that he was half in and half out, his hanging arms actually touching the water. In that position he might have been a seasick passenger consigning his dinner to the depths.

But it was what de Burca was engaged in that held Hennessy's troubled gaze. Whistling cheerfully between his teeth, he was busy tying the anchor to Jethro's left ankle, completely absorbed in his work like a man with a quota to complete before he knocked off and went home for his tea.

Knowing that the moment had finally come to act, Hennessy stepped out of the hatch like Billy the Kid, gun at the ready. He wondered if he could really say "Hands up" without his voice breaking into a squeak but he was saved the trouble when de Burca looked up and saw him hovering.

Only a slight narrowing of the eyes betrayed his surprise: he was a pretty cool dude, the same de Burca. Sitting back on his heels, he spread his hands wide, then indicated the reclining figure beside him.

"It's not as bad as it seems," he said. "I was only going to give him a ducking to teach him to keep his nose out of my business."

"And what business would that be?" Hennessy asked, trying to sound more confident than he felt.

"Gun-running," de Burca said, as naturally as if it were the truth. "On behalf of you know who up there."

Vaguely he nodded in what Hennessy supposed was the direction of the north.

"Come off it," Hennessy said, "I know what you're up to. Jethro told me all about it. It's drugs you're into, and you don't care a fig about anyone except yourself."

de Burca nodded, as though confirming to himself what he already knew. Slowly he stood up, holding his hands out wide from his body.

"Well, it looks like a stand-off," he said. "I've got to gamble on how willing you are to shoot that gun. Have you ever seen the damage a harpoon can do? In order to get it out you have to pull it through from the other side."

"You're the one who'll be doing the pulling, not me."

"True, but have you the guts to shoot me with it in the first place. Let's find out..."

He took a step forward, then another. Looking straight at him, he was trying to stare Hennessy down. Beneath their feet the deck heaved as the boat hit a wave.

"Why don't you give me the gun?" de Burca said coaxingly. "I've no axe to grind with you. If you want I'll leave yourself and Cosgrave off at some isolated part of the coast. It's no problem. Just so long as I've got an hour's headstart..."

He was now within a couple of yards of Hennessy and closing fast. A decision would have to be made, otherwise the initiative would be lost. To gain time, Hennessy took a step backwards, then another, but he had forgotten about the hatch behind him. To his horror, his feet suddenly found no purchase: he was treading on empty air.

With the inevitability of night following day he commenced his descent, the shock of it causing him to yell and his finger to release the trigger of the gun. Before his eyes went below the rim of the hatch he saw the harpoon snaking in de Burca's direction, then he forgot about everything except preserving himself from serious breakage as he plummeted down.

But he was an old hand at falling into holes and, as soon as he touched firm ground, he bent his legs and rolled. The fall knocked the breath out of him but otherwise did him little harm.

As soon as he could get some air into his lungs he was back up the ladder, ready to renew hostilities. He need not have bothered. In striving to get out of the way of the harpoon, de Burca had evidently stumbled, hit his head on the jamb of the wheelhouse door and knocked himself out. He was now lying on his back with an almost contented look on his face, a consequence possibly of his subconscious telling him that at least he had managed to avoid being transfixed by the metal bolt from the harpoon gun. Many's the whale would have been glad to be in his place. The bolt itself was harmlessly embedded in the architrave round the door.

Offering up a silent prayer of thanksgiving, Hennessy took hold of Jethro and pulled him back so that all of him was lying once more in the boat. Then he went forward into the deckhouse and propped himself up in the bucket seat in front of the instrument panel. The wheel was secured by strapping to keep the boat going in a straight line but where that straight line led to he knew not.

Slowly the realisation came to him that he was alone on the ocean, in a boat that he knew precious little about and with no one for company except two unconscious characters, one of whom he wished would wake up, while desiring the other most definitely not to.

Remembering the title of the Rolling Stones' single that had been playing at the fancy dress ball, he thought how appropriate the title was to his present situation. He was certainly caught between a rock and a hard place...

20

Superintendent Albert O'Donnelly, nicknamed "Big Al" by his less than respectful subordinates in the drugs squad, was in a bad mood. In his youth he had been a very active man, a champion bicycle racer and a hurler of inter-county standard. But successive promotions had conspired to tie him more and more to his office, and the consequence was that he had put on weight, begun to suffer problems with his feet and become very disinclined to travel any distance from the city of Dublin.

But now here he was, on the say-so of one of his least dependable constables, standing on a cold cement jetty in a God-forsaken spot hundreds of miles from base, stamping his feet, blowing into his hands, and trying not to think of what the elements were doing to the precarious state of his bowels. If Jethro Cosgrave were to turn up now, he thought, he'd strangle him with his bare hands.

The two local constables, who had conducted him to his present dreary situation, cowered further back on the pier, intimidated by his rank and by the ferocity of his temper. Only his driver, who was used to his moods, had the temerity to approach but he ignored the proffered plastic cup of coffee and instead sent a few more curses whirling off into the night sky.

Because of snide remarks by his superiors on the scarcity of convictions over the last couple of months, he had been particularly eager to make this present arrest. Cosgrave had assured him that it was a cast-iron case, with no possibilities of a slip-up. This de Burca had, literally, been getting away with murder for nearly two years now. No ordinary, common garden yobbo, he was in the worst traditions of the gentleman crook, spreading money copiously in bribes, hiring the best legal brains to preserve his immunity and he was, it was rumoured, in possession of information that allowed him to blackmail a certain high-up member of the government so that he would put in a word for him in the right quarters.

Although harbouring an amount of sympathy for ordinary Joe Soaps who were forced into a life of crime due to circumstances of upbringing or galloping poverty, O'Donnelly hated smoothies like de Burca with all his heart. It made his day when he could put the strong arm on such as he and this was one of the factors that had induced him to make the long trip down from Dublin.

Muttering under his breath, he walked back down the pier towards the two uniformed Gardai. As he approached, a clandestine cigarette butt went spiralling over the edge to fizz furtively in the water below but he decided to ignore it.

"Are you absolutely sure this is the right place?" he inquired from the constable nearest him. "You couldn't have made a mistake?"

"You've asked me that before, sir," the constable said plaintively. "The message we got was to conduct you to Trá Bhán at zero plus one hundred hours, there to await developments. This is Trá Bhán and the time is approximately…"

"Yes, I know, zero plus one hundred hours. It's one o'clock, why can't you say that like any normal sane person?" O'Donnelly gestured at the darkness all around them. "There's nothing happening," he said. "It's as quiet as a nursery at feeding time…"

"Well, it was your own man that gave us the message," the constable answered, not willing to be burdened with the blame for bringing such a big shot on what was possibly a wild-goose chase.

"My own man…"

O'Donnelly ground his teeth as though to demonstrate what he would do with his "own man" when he got hold of him. He was about to say more when he suddenly broke off and cocked his head into a listening attitude.

"D'you hear something?"

The three of them, plus the driver, strained their ears and, sure enough, a sound began to bleed its way into the silence. It was a distant drone, the throb of an engine that steadily increased in volume as they listened.

"It's a boat," the second constable said.

Throwing him a murderous glance, O'Donnelly said, "I know it's a boat. But whose boat? What boat?" He cupped his eyes and stared out over the water. "Bring up the car," he instructed his driver. "We'll put the spotlight on it."

The driver went away and in a short time he had manoeuvred the police car out onto the pier, the headlights causing them all to blink. When the spot blazed on, it was shining directly into the Superintendent's face.

"Not on me, you fool," he snarled, shielding his eyes. "Out in that direction."

He pointed to his right and the light obligingly poked off where he indicated. Very soon, though, it became apparent that his ears had been playing him tricks, for it was behind them that the side lights of the boat suddenly loomed, and with a rushing roar the craft came directly at the pier. When it seemed inevitable that it would score a bullseye, it abruptly slewed around broadside but its momentum caused it to continue on and crash resoundingly into the cement wall of the jetty.

The two constables and the driver were nimble on their feet and managed to leap clear but O'Donnelly's bulk hampered him, slowing him down. The result was that the tidal wave as the boat hit caught him in mid stride, and he went up in the air, over the side of the pier and disappeared with a tremendous splash into the icy waters of Trá Bhán.

"I couldn't find the brake," Hennessy said, causing the rest of the company to throw their eyes heavenward.

"If you say that one more time," Superintendent O'Donnelly said, "I'll have you thrown into the Bridewell and kept there for the rest of your natural existence."

They were back in the Tóin le Gaoith garda station, the two constables, the driver, a recovered Jethro Cosgrave and a very much on the defensive Hennessy. The still unconscious de Burca had been taken away by ambulance to Galway.

Jethro looked none the worse for wear but O'Donnelly was feeling very sorry for himself indeed. He was sitting wrapped in a blanket, his feet in a basin of hot water and his clothes steaming on a protesting radiator. After being fished out of the lagoon his temper had hit mark ten on the Richter scale, but he had calmed down slightly and was now merely rumbling like a minor Vesuvius.

"I can't think why you let yourself get into such a situation," he told Jethro. "And then having to be rescued by a midget pirate." He glanced with disgust at Hennessy. "Or whatever he's supposed to be."

"de Burca outsmarted me, that's all," Jethro said. "He's a smooth mover, full of street capability. I thought I was good but he was obviously better."

"The boat's a write-off," the driver put in with relish. "About two hundred thousand pounds worth."

"He'll get a good lawyer and sue us for that," O'Donnelly said gloomily. "Takes the good out of the collar."

"I just couldn't find the brake," Hennessy said again. "How was I supposed to know you pulled it instead of stepping on it?"

"Will you get him out of here." The Superintendent closed his eyes to show the pain he was in. "Take him home or back to his cage, or wherever he belongs. I don't want to see him again as long as I live."

"Come on," Jethro said, standing up. "I'll walk down the road with you. You can come in tomorrow and give a full statement. I think the boss wants to be alone..."

They went out, borne on the backwash of O'Donnelly's heated mutterings. "That's all the thanks I get," an angry Hennessy said, as they walked down the corridor. "I stop a well-known drugs dealer from getting away. I prevent a couple of murders. And do I get a reward for my troubles? No, instead I'm treated like a criminal myself..."

"I'm certainly grateful to you," Jethro said. "If you hadn't put your oar in, I'd be fish meat by now."

"Yeah, you would. Is there no quotation from the Bible that springs to mind?"

"Well, I'm reminded of the story of David and Goliath—I suppose you could be said to have slain the giant..."

Hennessy's face lit up. "Right on, man," he said, punching the air. "Right on."

It was the following Monday morning, classes were

out, and Hennessy was holding court outside the schoolhouse. Word of his escapades on the Saturday night had spread like wildfire and he was now a celebrity in his own right.

Earlier he had had a rather painful interview with Tommy Ugly, flanked by his second-in-command, Mr Ó Cadhla, at which he'd been warned as to his future conduct, told to mind his own business from now on and then been grudgingly commended for his derring-do.

Now he sat on the school wall, flanked by Brooks, Kitty and Elsie, and a subdued-looking Swift and O'Brien, who felt that their success on the musical scene should entitle them to some of the acclaim that was being spread about.

"Well," Brooks said, summing up all their feelings, "the next two weeks are going to be a bit of an anti-climax after what's just happened. Back to learning and sitting on an old hard bench..."

"Imagine Máistir de Burca being a drugs smuggler," Kitty said. "I thought he was dishy, with that big car and that boat."

"He was lovely," Elsie agreed. "He winked at me once and I was going around in a daze all day."

"What'd happen if I winked at you?" Brooks asked.

"You'd bring her outta the daze," Swift said.

The weather had cleared up again and the forecast was good: bright days with plenty of sun, mild nights with calm breezes. de Burca had already been replaced by a young, freckle-faced teacher with a pronounced Kerry accent who was so energetic there appeared to be two of him. He had a full schedule of activities lined up for them and they would have little time to bemoan any lack of excitement.

Hennessy was feeling on top of the world. The course had already satisfied his longing for adventure, Kitty was all over him again since he'd become famous and soon after his return to Dublin he'd be winging his way to Africa to see his father and mother and to renew his acquaintance with that beautiful and mysterious continent. God certainly seemed to be in his heaven and all was right with the world.

And at that very moment God's messenger, the old Bible-quoter himself, came tootling down the road on his motorbike. Drawing up beside them in a cloud of blue smoke, he stood astride the machine and eased back the visor of his helmet.

"Well, if it isn't the Knight of the Sad Countenance," Brooks greeted him. "Good morning, Don Quixote."

"Ola! Sancho Panza," Jethro said. "Go off and feed my donkey while I talk to these merry wasters..."

They grinned at him, and he grinned back. There was something about Jethro that would always make people feel good and cause them to smile at him. It was probably the sense of innocent fun that he radiated, which brought a realisation that although outwardly he might appear a buffoon there was still a well of goodness in his heart. One instinctively felt that in his company life would always be cheerful, full of surprises and never, never dull.

"Well, this is the parting of the ways, comrades," he said. "I've got to go off and tilt at a few more windmills and you've got to stay and learn your book..."

He leaned over and solemnly shook hands with each of them in turn. When Hennessy took his back he was holding a round metal object that glinted in the sun.

"The cap from my petrol tank," Jethro explained. "I thought you'd like to have it as a memento of your summer in the west. It makes me nervous even to look at it."

"Thanks," Hennessy said. "I'll keep it under my pillow at night and hope it doesn't explode."

"That's it, then," Jethro said, nodding. He kicked the starter and the engine spluttered into life.

As he was pulling down his visor, Hennessy suddenly asked him, "Haven't you any farewell quotation from the Bible for us?"

Jethro paused; then he said, "'Better is a handful of quietness than two hands full of toil and a striving after wind...' Ecclesiastes chapter 4: verse 6..."

For some reason they all turned and looked at Brooks, the phantom farter.

"There's only one response to that," Hennessy said. "Now all together..."

And they all chorused, "Amen."

Children's
POOLBEG

To get regular
information about
our books and authors join

THE POOLBEG
BOOK CLUB

Children's Poolbeg Books

Author	Title	ISBN	Price
Banville Vincent	Hennessy	1 85371 132 2	£3.99
Beckett Mary	Orla was Six	1 85371 047 4	£2.99
Beckett Mary	Orla at School	1 85371 157 8	£2.99
Comyns Michael	The Trouble with Marrows	1 85371 117 9	£2.99
Considine June	When the Luvenders came to Merrick Town	1 85371 055 5	£4.50
Considine June	Luvenders at the Old Mill	1 85371 115 2	£4.50
Considine June	Island of Luvenders	1 85371 149 7	£4.50
Corcoran Clodagh ed.	Baker's Dozen	1 85371 050 4	£3.50
Corcoran Clodagh ed.	Discoveries	1 85371 019 9	£4.99
Cruickshank Margrit	SKUNK and the Ozone Conspiracy	1 85371 067 9	£3.99
Cruickshank Margrit	SKUNK and the Splitting Earth	1 85371 119 5	£3.99
Daly Ita	Candy on the DART	1 85371 057 1	£2.99
Daly Ita	Candy and Sharon Olé	1 85371 159 4	£3.50
Dillon Eilís	The Seekers	1 85371 152 7	£3.50
Dillon Eilís	The Singing Cave	1 85371 153 5	£3.99
Duffy Robert	Children's Quizbook No.1	1 85371 020 2	£2.99
Duffy Robert	Children's Quizbook No.2	1 85371 052 0	£2.99
Duffy Robert	Children's Quizbook No.3	1 85371 099 7	£2.99
Duffy Robert	The Euroquiz Book	1 85371 151 9	£3.50
Ellis Brendan	Santa and the King of Starless Nights	1 85371 114 4	£2.99
Henning Ann	The Connemara Whirlwind	1 85371 079 2	£3.99
Henning Ann	The Connemara Stallion	1 85371 158 6	£3.99
Hickey Tony	Blanketland	1 85371 043 1	£2.99
Hickey Tony	Foodland	1 85371 075 X	£2.99
Hickey Tony	Legendland	1 85371 122 5	£3.50
Hickey Tony	Where is Joe?	1 85371 045 8	£3.99
Hickey Tony	Joe in the Middle	1 85371 021 0	£3.99
Hickey Tony	Joe on Holiday	1 85371 145 4	£3.50
Hickey Tony	Spike & the Professor	1 85371 039 3	£2.99
Hickey Tony	Spike and the Professor and Doreen at the Races	1 85371 089 X	£3.50
Hickey Tony	Spike, the Professor and Doreen in London	1 85371 130 6	£3.99
Kelly Eamon	The Bridge of Feathers	1 85371 053 9	£2.99
Lavin Mary	A Likely Story	1 85371 104 7	£2.99
Lynch Patricia	Brogeen and the Green Shoes	1 85371 051 2	£3.50
Lynch Patricia	Brogeen follows the Magic Tune	1 85371 022 9	£2.99
Lynch Patricia	Sally from Cork	1 85371 070 9	£3.99
Lynch Patricia	The Turfcutter's Donkey	1 85371 016 4	£3.99
MacMahon Bryan	Patsy-O	1 85371 036 9	£3.50
McCann Sean	Growing Things	1 85371 029 6	£2.99
McMahon Sean	The Poolbeg Book of Children's Verse	1 85371 080 6	£4.99
McMahon Sean	Shoes and Ships and Sealing Wax	1 85371 046 6	£2.99
McMahon Sean	The Light on Illancrone	1 85371 083 0	£3.50
McMahon Sean	The Three Seals	1 85371 148 9	£3.99
Mullen Michael	The Viking Princess	1 85371 015 6	£2.99
Mullen Michael	The Caravan	1 85371 074 1	£2.99
Mullen Michael	The Little Drummer Boy	1 85371 035 0	£2.99
Mullen Michael	The Long March	1 85371 109 8	£3.50
Mullen Michael	The Flight of the Earls	1 85371 146 2	£3.99
Ní Dhuibhne Eilís	The Uncommon Cormorant	1 85371 111 X	£2.99

While every effort is made to keep prices low, it is sometimes necessary to increase prices at short notice. Poolbeg Press Ltd reserves the right to show new retail prices on covers which may differ from those previously advertised in the text or elsewhere.

All Poolbeg books are available at your bookshop or newsagent or can be ordered from:

Poolbeg Press Knocksedan House
Forrest Great Swords Co Dublin
Tel: 01 407433 Fax: 01 403753

Please send a cheque or postal order (no currency) made payable to Poolbeg Press Ltd.

Allow 80p for postage for the first book, plus 50p for each additional book ordered.